My Personal History
My Story

My Personal History
My Story

TOWN & COUNTRY
PUBLIC LIBRARY DISTRICT
320 E. North Street
Elburn, IL 60119

Janice Costello

Copyright © 2016 by Janice Costello.

Library of Congress Control Number: 2016902037
ISBN: Hardcover   978-1-5144-4567-9
             Softcover   978-1-5144-4568-6
             eBook   978-1-5144-4569-3

All rights reserved. No part of this book may be reproduced or transmitted in any form or by any means, electronic or mechanical, including photocopying, recording, or by any information storage and retrieval system, without permission in writing from the copyright owner.

Any people depicted in stock imagery provided by Thinkstock are models, and such images are being used for illustrative purposes only.
Certain stock imagery © Thinkstock.

Print information available on the last page.

Rev. date: 04/01/2016

To order additional copies of this book, contact:
Xlibris
1-800-455-039
www.Xlibris.com.au
Orders@Xlibris.com.au
633178

This is Me — Who are You

I have written about events that I have in my life, how I coped with the ups and downs that life has thrown at me. Perhaps you would like to go on this journey with me, I have given heading to the stories, if you think about them you might have a story tucked away in some corner of your mind you could write about, some day your children or grandchildren may be interested in knowing who you were, what you felt like when you were young, your fascinations and frustrations, did you have dreams that motivated you. How your thinking changed over time.

Some of these will be incidences, others are complete stories in themselves, if they have a beginning a hint of what you are writing about. A middle which has information, the facts and figures what happened and an end where your reader knows when that story is finished. Some will just be odd things that have happened, however they are all things that have influenced my life. I have 3 sons, Greg, Paul and Brett, you will hear about them in some stories, but it will be mostly Brett and I as Greg and Paul had left home when a lot of these events happened. It was after the boys has left home that I had time to think about who am I? The journey I have been on has allowed me to grow as a person, in ways I could have never dreamt of.

In this first story, I am writing 'about a friendship, which only takes six lines, but if I want to make it more interesting, so that a reader appreciate what really happened, I need to have more detail which is in the second, attempt of writing 'about a friendship'

First Story

Write of a Friendship You Have Had

1. Write about a friendship or love you have had.

It is strange the way a friendship can start. I had—or should I say—our dogs met in the laneway. We immediately began to talk. She was very interesting, and when we came to my back gate off the laneway, I invited her for a cup of coffee. We sat on the back veranda as our dogs frolicked on the lawn. That was years ago, and we still see each other at least once a fortnight and talk about many things. Though we were quite different people, we seem to be able to have answers to each other's thoughts. And the dogs are still friends too.

2. Now show us that story, making it twice as long, by including, what I saw and thought, making you feel it more.

I looked at my dog and said, 'Walk.' That was all that was needed to be said. We headed for the back gate, the dog leaping and bounding around in circles. He wanted to go for a walk, but I should go for a walk; there was a big difference in our enthusiasm. Out in the laneway, there were no dogs or people, so I didn't put his lead on. It was a pleasant walk. Tall trees grew on either side of the track. They were casting shadowed patterns on the lush undergrowth beneath and on the track as the sun shone through the leaves. The air was fresh and clean, renewing my spirit.

Some birds swooped down on my dog; I guess they had a nest nearby. We could go 100 yards up the track. However, if the weather wasn't nice or if I didn't feel like it, we didn't go all the way. I mean, he was only a dog. A walk was a walk, wasn't it? This particular day, the weather was perfect, so we did the full walk. It was much nicer walking in the laneway than on the street. On the street, the houses and gardens were nice, but in the laneway, the trees were standing tall, and the leaves were swaying in the breeze, seemingly different, greener, less tortured by civilisation. It was like the whole place was alive. And let's not forget the most beautiful tree on the walk. Not actually in the laneway, it was just on the other side of the fence. It was an elm. Standing tall and proud, it reached up into the sky above the rest of the trees, its branches spreading wide and strong. The bright green leaves just knew they were privileged to be on such a majestic tree.

Oh, oh, there is someone coming. So I put the dog on his lead. The two dogs got closer and closer; neither seemed to be stressed, so they stood next to each other. The owner and I spoke. She was a little older than I was. She was neatly dressed and was still slim and attractive. We spoke, and that one sentence turned into another and another. We walked along side by side. She was very interesting, and when we came to my back gate off the laneway, I invited her for a cup of coffee.

We sat on the back veranda as our dogs frolicked on the lawn. Being with a person so different from me, I'd found it opened my mind to a lot of things I would never have thought about. Perhaps we shouldn't just seek to be friends with people we seem to have similar interests with as they will only mirror our own views.

That was years ago. We still see each other at least once a fortnight and talk and laugh about many things. The dogs remained friends too. Isn't it strange the way a friendship can start?

* * *

Don't start with 'I was born'. Choose an outstanding moment and then reflect back. Instead, you can say, 'When I was five, I got knocked down by a car and had a broken leg and a fractured skull.' Or instead I could say, 'My life was going well until a car came along and nearly wiped my life out of existence.'

I would like to tell you about early recollections in my life. The heading is 'As I Remember It'. Then comes the middle, with my thoughts and happenings, and then finishing. I want to leave it where it sounds like I've finished. Sometimes there might be a theme or a particular setting or a plot. I would like you to think about my theme or setting and try to recall a similar situation.

Each of us has three resources to get us through the day—time, energy, and the power of our minds.

Our brain works by the following:

- programming—creates beliefs
- beliefs—create attitudes
- attitudes—create feelings
- feelings—determine action
- actions—create results.

No one will ever think the thought that is ours. No one will ever stand in our bodies, experience what has happened to us, feel our fears, dream our dreams, or cry our tears. We are born, live, and leave this life entirely on our own. I hope in your writing you can see that at times you have taken responsibility and that, with positive actions, you can see that at times you were consciously in charge—though when writing about an incident when we were children, it was out of our control and it just happened.

The second story holds memories of growing up, early recollections

Second Story

As I Remember It: Growing Up on Mackie Road, East Bentleigh

As I lay unconscious in the hallway of the hospital, my skull fractured and leg broken, my life was hanging in the balance. I was unaware of my fragile grasp on life. My parents and the local doctor frantically hovered over the hospital trolley. The rain outside was pelting relentlessly against the hospital windowpanes. The doctor said, 'Let's get her out of here. If we leave her here, she'll die before she gets seen!' When I awoke, my head was bandaged, and my leg, mummified in plaster, was suspended in the air. I had not known that I had knocked on death's door.

Up until this time, my life had been going along just fine on my parents' market garden property about six kilometres out of Bentleigh. People had said to Dad, 'You are mad going to live right out there. Nobody will ever live that far from Bentleigh.' There were about seven houses that could be seen from our land. All you could really see were endless market gardens.

There were no local shops; the bread man came about every third day on a horse and cart. The ice man came once a week. By the time the week was up, there would be just a tiny slither of ice that hadn't melted in the icebox—no refrigeration then.

On market day, my father would get up at 4 a.m. to go to the market. Sometimes I would hear him walking out of the house, his footsteps slowly disappearing, being swallowed up by the night. He sold his produce to the people that you would buy your vegetables from if you went to buy at the market. My father would take me once a year during the school holidays. It was so exciting getting up in the dark and seeing market stall holders going from truck to truck, looking for the produce that looked the best to them. And then, we would go across the road and buy breakfast, sausages and eggs, which to me was just so exotic. Then one year, dad didn't wake me; he'd gone without me. I was devastated; I had thrown my face into my pillow and burst into passionate sobbing.

My grandfather was also a market gardener, and in his earlier days, he would go by horse and cart to the market, the only advantage being that, as the horse jogged along, the rhythm of the hooves on the road lulled my grandpa to sleep. It wasn't a problem as the horse knew its way to the South Melbourne Market. My grandfather also had a cantankerous horse who didn't like people very much. He would be attached to a buggy, and if any of the men tried to get in the buggy, he would just take off before they could get a foothold. With my grandmother, it would wait until she got on board and then take off at tremendous speed.

My brother, two years older than me, had a friend over the road. We would spend a lot of time on the properties. My sister, four years younger, was not part of these adventures as she was home with Mum, and she can't remember playing in the paddocks. The blossom trees around the house were musical with bees. There were numerous fruit trees —a fig tree, a peach tree, an apricot tree, two cooking apple trees, two lemon trees, a pomegranate, and even a guava tree. They were all prolific except the peach tree; it never really got the hang of having fruit.

From these, my mother would bottle the fruit, so we had lovely desserts all year, and let's not forget the jams. My mother also made cakes and biscuits. There were lovely aromas coming out of our kitchen many times as I came home from school. We ate well. After strenuous days of play, we champed and chewed and relished our food, never really giving much thought to the effort Mum had put into our meals.

In our backyard was a big willow tree. When we were old enough, my brother and I each took a hessian bag each from the shed and climbed the willow tree like we often did, climbing the branches like a ladder. And with a hammer and nails, we each nailed our bags into the forks of the tree on opposite sides. On hot days, we would go up there with comics and read, reclining in our handmade hammocks; on a hot day, it was much cooler up there. Our hair would have a golden glow as the sun filtered through the leaves of the tree. With a twig of the tree, we swished the flies away.

As children, we played in our yard on the soft grass, running around the house with the energy of youth, the cloudless summer sky holding hours of daylight for us. We made mud pies. We jumped over the furrows; how high we had to jump depended on what was growing in them. We jumped over nettles, daisies, and dandelions, and we collected pieces of china from the workmen's broken cups. We played marbles or jacks with knuckle bones from the roast lamb, and we would laugh over nothing as children tended to do. There was plenty to do, or there was nothing—whatever we felt like.

The summer passed with days beginning to shorten, and as the days rolled by slowly, summer blended into autumn. On warms days, we played in the rain, and we would return home happily with wet hair plastered to our heads and water dripping down our backs. As I got older, the willow tree was used less and less. One time I hadn't been up there for about six months, and on getting up there, I shook the bag to shake the leaves out. To my shock, a possum jumped out. I can tell you that was the last time I went up there.

What did I learn when I was young? I learned that tadpoles wouldn't turn into frogs or anything else if you put them in a tin container. I learned that if I climbed the pear tree over the road with my brother and his mate and called out 'You've got a flat tyre', someone might just stop and we had to jump down from the pear tree and run for our lives. I learned, if my brother told me, to ask for Tudor Street when I got on the bus after school that I shouldn't insist that I lived on Mackie Road because if that was what I asked for, when we got to Mackie Road, the bus, with a grinding scrape of the brakes, would pull up at the kerb and the driver would turn around and, with a loud booming voice that reached the back of the bus, say, 'This is your stop.' Feeling about twenty centimetres tall and absolutely embarrassed, I would have to say, 'I want the next stop please.'

Barry, my brother had a sleep-out which was built on to the house. There was a fernery extending out from that. I hated thunder and lightning storms, as I suppose most children did, and I used to sit in the middle of the room, thinking that was the safest place. Mum asked me to go out and shut Barry's window one stormy day. The grey clouds were swirling in the sky, the lightning flashing. I stood at the back door, trying to gauge the right time to run the few feet to Barry's door. I made it; the screen door banged behind me from the wind. Then on getting back, I was just about to grab the back door when, *flash*. The lightning was so close to me that everything went red, with little flashing stars everywhere. It was the only time I could remember screaming. This did not improve my opinion of thunder and lightning storms. Years later, lightning hit the willow tree and split it in half. With a shivering groan, half of the tree fell. Fortunately, the half that fell did not go in the direction of the house.

At one stage, I wanted to grow some vegetables like my father, so I planted turnips. When they were about 3 centimetres high, my dad said, 'You have to thin them out now, just leave one every ten centimetres and throw the rest away.' 'I'm not throwing them away,' I said. 'I'll transplant them.' Dad said it wouldn't work, but it was reasonably successful. I don't even like turnips, but they are pretty, aren't they?

Oh yes, I nearly forgot to mention why I was in the hospital in a partially mummified state. Well, I can't really remember what happened, but I have to admit it was my fault. I mean, the car was meant to be on the road, not me. I had evidently run out to the road after I had heard a relative was about to arrive. I have no memory of the event nor memory of a lot that happened before then. For example, I cannot remember attending school before the accident. I have always felt lucky to be alive.

My parents were both placid people. They stayed married until death intervened. I can hardly remember them arguing. We grew up in a stable, happy home. Later in life, I heard people talking and saying, 'We were rich' or 'We were poor'. I don't recall being aware of such thoughts. We definitely weren't rich, but we never felt poor. There was no TV to show us all the things that we could have. They were doing the best that they could. We were so consumed with our own lives we didn't give a thought to the fact that they were actually living their lives too. We went away camping each year, which was a highlight of each Christmas. We had all that we needed.

Said because and very

Watch out for *because*. It's often not necessary—e.g. 'I went to the shop *because* I needed something' is better as 'I went to the shop, I needed something'. 'I detest her *because* she's a bitch' is better as 'I detest her, she's a bitch'. 'Veronica bought whole wheat bread *because* she is having a luncheon' is better as 'Veronica bought whole wheat bread, she is having a luncheon'.

Also watch out for the word *very*. To say: 'The boy was very noisy' doesn't add that much more to just saying 'The boy is noisy'.

And also watch out for the word *really*. 'It was really fine' doesn't help much to 'It was fine'.

The next stories. The first story will tell of obstacles that will try to prevent you from reaching your goal. The second will again show by using your imagination you recall much more of what happened.

1st Story

Did anyone try to talk you out of doing something you wanted to do?

Second Story

One or more instances that bring out what you saw, tasted, smelt, heard, or touched. Mine are on the lounge room, the laundry, ploughing . . . You can choose any room or incident.

* * *

If you're wanting to publish, you need an opening page, a closing page, and a synopsis of what each chapter is about. Depending on your story, an outline is like a synopsis.

A short story is 2,000 words long, so you can't spend 1,500 words setting up the scene. You may find that when you get to the end, you can cut the first paragraph right down. Your first sentence is very important.

For style, the word *said* is an example. Some writers go to a lot of trouble to avoid using this simple *verb*, alternatively using *bawled*, *gritted*, *complained*, *snorted*, *sighed*, *mumbled*, or *confided*.

The *theme* is the soul of the book, the reason you are writing it. Keep your eye on the peripheral characters. If, you are writing about events in your life, don't let one of the other characters take over and become the centre of attention.

By living in the moment, we are aware of our daily acts; they can take on new meaning as we discover we are not just machines. Life is not orderly. No matter how we try to make life so, right in the middle, someone breaks a leg, falls in love, or drops a jar of apple sauce. The mind is raw, full of energy, alive, and hungry. I do not think in the way we were bought up to think—well mannered, congenial.

Be specific—not *car* but *Nissen*, not *fruit* but *strawberry*, not *bird* but *magpie*, not 'a codependent, neurotic man' but 'Fred, who runs to turn on the stove for his wife, thinking she wants to make coffee, when she is heading for the refrigerator for a cool drink'.

Don't get hung up on punctuation, spelling, grammar; they can be fixed later.

If something scary comes up, go for it, go for the jugular. Hemingway said, 'Write hard and clear about what hurts, don't avoid it. It has energy.'

First Story

Did anyone try to talk you out of something you wanted to do? Like writing, I have read of ways to write, like getting up at a certain hour or setting aside a large quantity of time each day to write or even going to a cafe where you can sit and ponder while sipping your coffee, knowing you won't be interrupted by the phone or tempted to do other things.

However, in his book *Like the Flowing River*, Paulo Coelho puts a different slant on the process, giving seven insights to a writer along the lines of the following:

1. A writer always wears glasses. Even on a dull day, he wears dark glasses to make himself look impressive. He never combs his hair. Thought to looking so tired from writing, he doesn't care. It can hang in braids down his back, with wisps of hair seeming to have a mind of their own, hanging down over his face. He looks angry or depressed from the pressures of life and hangs around bars with other people, his eyes clear but shadowed with fatigue. An air of uncertainty hangs in the air in the bar. Some have thin worried smiles on their faces, while other people try to find their ways in life. He has ideas spinning around in his head, which are going to be in his next novel. All are as about as happy as they can be.

2. He is not meant to be understood by his fellow man, so he can act and speak as he likes, sure of the fact that he has been born into the wrong lifetime. He tirelessly writes and rewrites his sentences, hating the thought that another writer has done better than him. But he walks and talks as if he owns the world.

3. He feels only understood by another writer, someone else with a creative mind, someone else who is aware that life is ticking away, marking the increments in his life. But he also hates other writers, hoping they have not the desire, focus, and courage that will lead to success or the brilliant ideas he has for his next book. Each writer tries to learn the others' secrets but giving away none of their own.

4. He can seduce a woman with memorised quotes from other authors and by scribbling on the woman's napkin at the table some luring, endearing message so she will hold that memory forever.

5. Once a recognised writer, he can always get a job as a literary critic, where he must analyse the writings of others. To make himself look important, he will include words like the *epistemological cut* or *integrated bi-dimensional vision of life*, saying nice things about his friends, which in turn makes him look good. People will think, *What an educated man*. His words can also become slurred. The audience will just think he's had many sleepless nights, trying to put ingenious thoughts together. But they won't buy the book as they will be afraid they will not understand it once they come to the epistemological cut. ·

6. When asked what he is reading at the moment, he will create there on the spot some strange name, referring to a book that doesn't even exist.

7. When asked whom he admires, he will say '*Ulysses* by James Joyce', knowing nobody would refute him even though they have probably never read it. You can talk about anything or nothing because

behind it all, people think that great thoughts go on inside your head.

Armed with this information, he went to his mother and explained exactly what a writer was. She was somewhat surprised. But she was relentless in her efforts to stop him from wasting his life being a writer.

Twice, his family had him put in a mental asylum, trying to show how insane it was to write a book. Turns out one of his books is very insightful—about mental patients.

However, he is successful selling millions of books. He is putting money into opening an orphanage and doing other helpful thing in his South American countries.

Second Story

These next stories are about, our lounge room, our horse, and our laundry. They are memories partly because of my 5 senses – what I saw, heard, smelt, tasted and felt. Similar to this poem.

Poem

With the touch of the wind, the grasses swish
Flags slap and snap at the sky
With the touch of the wind, the treetops sigh
It thumps the branches with its hand
And dead branches come tumbling down with a crash
The acorns roll, and the withered leaves get kicked about.

The Lounge Room

Many cold nights were spent in the lounge room. On Sundays, Barry and I would sit on the floor, glued to the radio in front us. We'd listen to Daddy and Paddy or to Biggles and Berty, the suspense building as the show drew to an end. Biggles's plane had been shot, and in the process of plummeting to the ground, there were sound effects that left us in no doubt what was happening. And then, of course, at the most suspenseful moment, we were told that was the end of the show for that week. So we had to wait in suspense until the next week to hear if Biggles lived.

During this time, my father was down on one knee, coaxing the ember in the fire grate to ignite the new wood he had put on. The wood was damp, so it was hissing and spitting. Paper was torn up and added, and the flame would flare up. The smoke was drawn up the chimney and snatched away by the wind. With a brass poker, Dad rearranged the logs that were now snarling and throwing out showers of sparks up into the blackened chimney.

On the mantelpiece, a clock ticked away. Outside, the wind-driven rain beat furiously against the glass windowpane. By now, the fire was dancing in the grate, and the room was warming up. Mum was sitting on the sofa, her knitting needles furiously clicking away, and the cat was in quiet contentment near the fire. Dad sometimes played his banjo mandolin. We were cosy and warm though still conscious of the cold drafts squeezing under the closed door.

Ploughing

In the early morning, Dad led the horse out to the paddock, with all her jangling bits, to be connected to the plough. The horse was brown and big-boned, for she was a draught horse. She'd then dip her head, breath steaming from her widened nostrils drooped in the frosty air. When Dad was ready, she pulled the plough. It was her job, and she was proud of it. With blinkers on and the single furrow plough attached, she walked her straight line, the plodding sound of the horse's hooves joining with the other sounds.

Dad never looked down to the ground when ploughing. He would look to where he needed to end up. It might have been a tree at the end of the paddock. Many times, both Dad and the horse trudged through a quagmire of mud. Despite the growing heat of the day, the ground was still mushy from the storm a few days earlier. By the end of the day, the horse's hair was rough and streaked and matted with dust and sweat. After her day, Dad would give her a carrot, and she would neigh with quivering nostrils.

The Laundry

Thursday was washing day, and it did take most of the day. First, a fire had to be lit under the copper. Gradually, the water grew hot and began to froth and bubble from the soap and the heat, and the washing would begin.

Mum would stir the copper with a long wooden pole. Then the sheets and everything else had to be hauled into one side of the double cement troughs and put through the wringer, then rinsed, and again put through the wringer, threading the items through the rollers to squeeze the water out. The clothes would then end up in the other trough. Finally, the washing was put out on the line to be blown dry by the wind. I could see the sheets, towels, and clothes on the line dancing with the wind, the sheet snapping like flags.

Women today would nearly die, saying, 'You mean I can't put the washing on while the kids are having breakfast and have it finished when I get back after taking them to school. It was very different then, but Mum was a happily married woman, totally preoccupied by the narrow confines of life in the forties and fifties.

Even nature finds a way of expressing itself

Poem

The sea has a voice that murmurs all day,
and all through the night in a soft, secret way.
But when it is angry, its voice is a roar
that thunders and booms as it reaches the shore.
The wind has a voice that whistles and sighs
and whispers a story and sings lullabies.
But just like the sea, when angry, it roars,
rattles windows, and slams doors.
So many voices you hear everywhere,
some close to ground, some in the air.
Whenever you hear them, you must listen well.
I'm sure all the voices have something to tell.

First Story

What did you attempt to do that was doomed to fail?

Second Story

Write about a life experience, a time when things were looking bad but you managed to get through it triumphantly, smart enough to get out of a sticky situation.

* * *

Luck is just the intersections of two roads—preparation and opportunity.
You are who you think you are, not what you're told you are.

There are Five Elements of Writing

There are five basic elements to writing: plot, characters, theme, setting, and background or style. They won't all be important in every given story; usually, one will be dominant.

1. The *plot* is simply what happens in the story. The most complicated plots occur in detective stories, but most are very simple and depend on other facts to bring the story to life in the reader's mind.

2. *Characters* bring depth to the participants in a story, showing their personalities and making them recognisable to the reader or listener. It may be in conversational bit or telling of movement, temperament, and reactions to different situations.

3. The *theme* is the main point of a story. A theme doesn't need to be explained; it just unfolds as the story is presented.

4. The *setting* means the place and time in which the story occurs; it may be in a ballroom, the jungle, a spaceship, or the streets of Melbourne. It's the backdrop to your story, often setting the feeling and creating the mood suited to the action of the story.

5. The *style* refers to the manner in which the writer tells the story, the techniques he or she uses to convey the story to the reader. There are several questions you can ask yourself when reading to identify the style of any particular writer.

How Is the Story Being Told?

What tense is the story written in? What sort of language is used? Is the story told through narration or dialogue or a combination of both?

Short sharp sentences can emphasise dramatic action or tension. *Long sentences* can be more emotional and reflective, descriptive passages full of imagery to build a lead or situation slowly towards a climax.

Who Is Telling the Story (the Author's Place in the Story)?

1. If you are telling it as yourself being the first person, the story is told only as that person's point of view.

2. Novels are usually written using a third-person point of view. This way, they can tell you what is going on in the mind of each character.

Techniques of Writers

- A flashback takes you into the past and then brings you smoothly back to the present.
- There may be a common link between paragraphs, which helps the story run in a continuous flow through each chapter.
- There can be a seed of an idea that grows and develops as time goes by.
- There can be a twist at the end. This most often happens when there is a seed of an idea developing through the story. The theme that has been developing is whipped from under you, possible changing your whole view of the story.
- Characters can be developed by their dialogue.
- Gestures reoccurring in a character can help identify them without needing long explanations.
- The repetition of a word or idea can be used deliberately to good effect.
- The story can be told in chronological order, logically right from the beginning.

- A 'slice of life' story has no build-up and ends abruptly, leaving the reader to think about further possibilities.
- A short story can be 500 words. At 1,500 words above that, it becomes a novelette.

First Story

I Should Have Told Him

I should have told him. I know I should have. I mean, just how difficult can it be to ride a horse? I looked at the horse uncertainly, and he looked at me with mischief in his eyes. I do know I should get on from the left side, and I could surely sit in that great big saddle. Hmm . . . I really needed some steps to be able to get my foot in the stirrup.

The owner really should have twigged that I had zero experience. However, once up, I sat there with a tiny nervous smile on my face. My, I was so high up off the ground.

The breeze blew my hair, like when an experienced rider glided through the air with the horse in full stride, a picture of harmony with nature. However, when we moved, all harmony disappeared. Why were some riders just sticking to their saddles, whereas myself and some others were bouncing all over the place?

At times, the really experienced people rode off, leaning forward with anticipation on their faces for the thrill of the ride. The horses raced, pumping adrenaline through their veins, their manes and tails flying in the air, their nostrils flared, looking as though they loved it.

My horse was not going to experience that today. When the ordeal was finally over, I dismounted. It would have been handy to know that I had to take my left foot out of the stirrup before sliding off instead of falling into the mud, having one foot still stuck in the stirrup. Next time, I would tell them I was inexperienced, but I wouldn't need to. There would not be a next time.

Second Story

Alone on the Hill: Getting Out of a Sticky Situation

The air was clean. The hills were densely covered with trees. There were mountains in the distance. We were set for a break. We were at a property that was owned at the time by Waverley Industries. It was off the main road from Warrigal, 100 kilometres from Melbourne.

On occasions, we had working bees. Parents and employees who could spare the time for the weekend would go and help clean up the place. The property covered over 20 hectares and consisted of undulating rural land, mostly uncleared, with a large lake hidden away down at the end of the track. There was even a small pine forest. The landscape was lush and green and wild.

A short distance from the entrance to the property just along the dirt driveway was a house, and over the other side of the driveway was a games room, where lots of fun was had. But this was not where we stayed. Still in our car, we headed up the rather steep hill, and turning right near the top, we then came to the cabins. There were about a dozen self-contained cabins up there, all sitting on the side of the steep hill. The panoramic view was fantastic. I think they had previously been used in the snow season. The property was now being used for holiday breaks for Waverley Industries employees and their families.

Brett and I had been up on working bees and just loved the place. In the mornings, we would be woken to spectacular sunrises even though the last remnants of mist hung like smoke in the lower hills. The place gave me a sense of expectancy, joy, and freedom. Those were the kind of sunrises that stirred the soul.

Seeing we didn't have any plans for Christmas, we decided to go up there for a break. We took another boy from work with us too. He worked at Waverley Industries and, having a few problems at home, had been boarding with us for a short time. Brett and I stayed in the first cabin, and the other lad chose to stay in the fourth cabin. There were plenty of things for the boys to do. Brett chose to sleep next to the window. He said he wanted to see the sunrise and the horses when he first woke up in the morning.

A neighbouring farmer had six horses on the property, one of which was a Clydesdale. Brett thought the Clydesdale was just the most beautiful horse. But it didn't matter. Whichever angle I looked at it, I couldn't see it. There was also a rooster. I'm not sure who he belonged to, but during the day, he just walked in and around the horses' legs continually. I guess he had realised that this was the safest place when foxes were around.

Brett and the other boy would in the mornings walk down the hill towards the main house and feed the horses. Of course, it did not take long for the horses to know that the place to be in the morning was at the top corner of the paddock. Later in the day, Brett and the other boy would continue down this steep track past the two dams, past the small plum orchard that was behind the main house, and over to the games room to play table tennis. I tried not to do this trek more than once a day as the going down was so steep that it was not actually a pleasure and climbing back up the hill to the cabins was no fun at all.

We were quite alone up there. I'm not sure how near the next neighbour was. We certainly couldn't see any houses around. The first few nights, we were a touch uneasy at being alone and isolated on the hill. At night with the door closed, everything got quiet, the night even swallowing up the hills around us. There were times when a little bit of fear had to be held back—not from what we saw, but from what we heard and felt from noises outside the cabin, like the snap of dry twigs beneath the footsteps of a not-so-small animal. The front gate was locked so no car could come in, but a person could easily come in. Then I thought about the steep hill they would have to climb and decided that they would be too exhausted to be dangerous.

Many of the days were very hot. We didn't swim in the dam as within two steps, the water was out of our depth. But the dams were used; there was a little rowing boat which Brett used. The other boy didn't seem to like the water because there were leeches in the dam. I was not so much in the water but rather on it. Brett was in the boat, and I was lying on a lilo. Brett threw me a rope and pulled me around the dam. Now, how was that for living?

One day on returning to the cabin, Brett stopped to feed the horses while I went ahead to change. I entered the cabin and then thought I should hang the wet towel outside. While I was doing this, the door blew shut. Oh dear, I didn't have the key. I was alone on the hill. As I said, I didn't know where the next neighbour was. There was a phone in the house at the bottom of the hill, but the key to the house was in the cabin, as were the car keys and the gate key. I looked at the cabin. There was only a small window that was accessible. I called Brett up as he was the only one who could fit through the window.

I pulled out the rubber from around the edge of the window to get the wire and then the louvres out. Brett tried to get in but just couldn't manage to because of the height of the window; he said if he had a ladder, he could. So I went into the next cabin, which was open. With a knife from the kitchen drawer, I unscrewed the ladder from the double bunk, and Brett, leaning the ladder against the wall, climbed up and got in. Once the door was opened, I then put the louvres back in and pushed all the rubber back along the wire's edge. You wouldn't have known anything had happened. I was invincible.

During this episode, the other boy was asleep in his cabin. Thank goodness. I could just see in a (hopefully not) future court case, him saying 'Well, Mrs Costello showed me how easy it was to break in.'

My sister came up on the weekend. She was concerned that we weren't boiling the water before we drank it. I said, 'It's okay.' To that, she responded, 'What are you going to do, leave a note next to your dead body, saying "Don't drink the water"?' We went to a little country pub for dinner, but before we left, I hit my head on the metal bar of the top bunk as I stood up, a bit painful. But after we'd knocked off a carafe of wine, it was a matter of 'What head?'

During their time up there, while the boys were walking, they had seen a deer in the pine forest and an echidna at the lake. And as we were leaving, a kangaroo crossed the track in front of the car. The property was called Christmas Pines, but Brett thought it should have been called heaven.

Think also about the rhythm and the punctuation

First Story

How have you coped with a mishap in your life? Mine is on waiting on RACV outside Sam's Warehouse.

Second Story

Talk about an event that has happened in your life time that was astounding at the time. Mine is on Cyclone Tracy.

* * *

I had a little tea party
This afternoon at three
In all there were just three guests
I, myself, and me

I ate all the sandwiches
And myself drank all the tea
And all the cakes upon the plate
Were eaten up by me.

Rhythm and Punctuation

The following is from 'War song of the Saracens' by James Elroy Flecker (printed 1963, *Poetry Workshop*, a book used in year 10):

[1] We are they who come faster than fate: we are they who ride early or late:

[2] We storm at your ivory gate: Pale Kings of the sunset beware!

[3] Not in silk nor in samet we lie, nor in curtained solemnity die

[4] Among women who chatter and cry and children who mumble a prayer

[5] But we sleep by the ropes of the camp, and we rise with a shout and we tramp

[6] With the sun or the moon for a lamp, and the spray of the wind in our hair

At first, this poem didn't catch my attention at all, but if you (*a*) have the first two lines read by *men*, (*b*) the second two lines read by *women*, (*c*) the last two lines read by *both*, it makes more sense.

Notice the *regular pause* in the middle of each line. The thinking changed. In line 2, he is telling us what they are doing. After the pause, he tells us whom we should be aware of. In the fourth line, *there isn't a pause*; the same thought is carried through the whole line. In the fifth line, he tells us where they are. After the pause, he tells us when and what will happen.

Children, will understand rhythm before they understand words. We read storybooks to tiny children.

> Mary had a little lamb
> It's fleece was white as snow
> And everywhere that Mary went
> The lamb was sure to go.

Children let us tell them the story, but they are picking up and understanding the rhythm more than the words. Then comes the listening for the matching sounds of words. Primitive people move to their tribal dances; teenagers twist to the latest music.

It can be a jaunty regularity or a sobering saga. The *sound and repetition* sweep the poem along. It can soothe your restless spirit or stir your emotions.

Then again, we could put a different slant on the poem and break it into three parts.

First Story

One day I was outside Sam's Warehouse. I looked at the sky. It was so blue, with beautiful, fluffy white clouds and some very dark ones that had passed. The next dark clouds would be right over me in ten minutes. I hoped the RACV would come before then; though they did say they would be one hour. Why did I need the RACV? Well, I had just locked my keys in the boot of my car. I never put my keys in the boot, and I always unlock the doors first when I open the boot—except today that is.

I had such a nice morning, with a visit from a friend in the next street. Maybe I was thinking about the great conversation we had. As I was saying, the sky above was such a vivid blue, and the distant sky past the clouds was a softer, really beautiful colour. Maybe it was like the saying 'The grass is greener over next door'. The lighter colour of the sky was probably like that, with the haze floating in the atmosphere, whereas the sky above me was a powerful cobalt blue; it was real.

The situation I was in was real too. I didn't panic, thought it through, walked over the road to Rowville shops, bought a camping chair for $7.00 and a cookbook for $4.95 and then two tuna-and-rice sushi rolls and a Coke, and went back to my car. I sat in the chair behind my car for over an hour, patiently waiting, sitting, eating, and reading in the gentle breeze on a warm autumn day. People walked past, but I paid them no mind as they wondered what the crazy woman was doing. It was an awkward situation, but with all the stressful things that had happened in my life, this was nothing.

Second Story

An Australian Historical Event That Happened in Your Lifetime

While living in Port Moresby, the main town of Papua New Guinea, I had some interesting events, like when I was swimming in the ocean, I think my swimming ability would have been close to Olympic standards the day I saw a sea snake swimming near me. And let's not forget the day I was on the veranda and my two-year-old son was on the lawn just metres away, the problem being the snake at the bottom step, which was between us. But on the whole, living in Papua New Guinea had lots of good points. Port Moresby was really enjoyable when we only had Greg, our first child.

We lived on the outskirts of town, which was six kilometres out of Port Moresby—no traffic lights and one crossroad between the town and our place. It took usually six to seven minutes for John to get to work. Many a day, I would go to Ela Beach before lunch, and John would walk from work and have lunch with us. Oh, it was good, the sea breeze making it a perfect day. Of course, when the twins came just two years and three months later, it wasn't so easy; in fact, it became impossible within six months to look after the twins and chase a three-year-old runaway on the beach. Obedience wasn't one of his finest qualities. But this event that happened in 1974 could not be forgotten.

Houses in New Guinea were similar to houses in Darwin, mostly built up on stilts with louvre windows going from floor to ceiling to catch any breeze that you could get to relieve you from the constant hot, humid weather during the day. There were some built on the ground, and ever some like our house with a flat roof so the house heated like an oven.

And then, to our great surprise, a few days before Christmas in 1974, Cyclone Tracy let us know she was near. She hovered over the ocean between Australia and New Guinea for days; she didn't know which direction to go. While she was making up her mind, for days one hour before midnight, these ferocious winds would come. The curtain that usually hung from floor to ceiling would be thrust up by the winds and appear to be glued to the ceiling. The wind only lasted three to four minutes, and then as quickly as it came, it went, leaving complete calm.

Australia and New Guinea had been warned ten days before about the cyclone, but it didn't eventuate, so the next warning was taken with a blasé attitude. We in New Guinea were hoping it wouldn't come our way though we had absolutely no idea of the magnitude of a cyclone.

Then, on Christmas Eve, Cyclone Tracy struck, destroying Darwin in a few hours, leaving almost nothing standing. Darwin was a city no more. At the airport, winds were recorded at 217 kilometres an hour. They said it got to 300 kilometres an hour, but at the airport, the equipment measuring the wind speed itself had been blown away. At the time, the population of Darwin was 45,000 but was reduced to 10,000 because people had been told to leave days before. People scattered to Adelaide, Whyalla, Alice Spring, and Sydney. There were 20,000 left homeless. Many that left never came back. There was as much damage done as there was when Darwin was bombed in 1942.

Tracy's damage amounted to $837 million though it only spanned forty-eight kilometres; few cyclones were so compact. Most people in their homes pulled their strong metal-framed double beds to the centre of the room and got under them—this was what they had been instructed to do—while pieces of their houses disintegrated and flew away in the wind or landed on the bed. Seventy-one people died—forty-nine on land and twenty-two out at sea. Cyclone Tracy was classed as category 3.

One lady wrote that she had lost an arm and all Christmas presents just disappeared. And she said, 'My husband, who had gone to the shops for milk just before Tracy struck, was never seen again.' And her dog—well, two years later in Sydney—still howled in storms. I met a woman in Melbourne two years later when I was visiting her sister; she had been unable to resume her married life and was still having psychiatric treatment.

It took four years to rebuild houses, and all houses had a safe room—the bathroom, made of solid wall and just a very, very small window high on the wall. Sixty per cent of Darwin's 1974 population were not living in Darwin in 1980.

In 1974, as we awoke one hour before midnight on nights with the scary gigantic winds, we had no idea of the magnitude of destruction that was about to happen to Darwin. Darwin ceased to exist as a city, and Santa didn't go to Darwin in 1974.

Think about the Movement that is going on it needs to be explanation.

First Story

The Dining Room Table

Second Story

Write of a time as a child when you felt you were doing something common but felt you learned something new.

* * *

Men use *logic* more than women. Men traditionally work in groups, so there needs to be a communal logic, whereas women tend to work alone, so logic is not important.

Women use *intuition* much more. Logic is step by step; logic leads to a conclusion. Intuition is processing to reach a conclusion. To work on your own, you need only possibilities.

Example of Education on Movement

In this whole paragraph, only *four words* are spoken.

> I didn't look up from my book even though I did hear Paul approach. I looked up when Paul pulled out the chair, placed his coffee on the table and then sat with hands clasped on the table. He leaned towards me and

asked, 'How'd your day go?' I turned another page of the book, my mind running through my options of what to say. Paul took a sip of his coffee, put down the cup, and wiped the corners of his mouth with the thumb and forefinger of his right hand before he fixed his gaze on me. I was still pretending I was reading. I wanted to tell him to get lost.

Life is just a series of mostly forgettable events unless we love and love in as many different ways as we can—from loving a person, a book, a spirit, a place, an idea, or a dog to loving almost anything. It's those moments when we feel connected to someone or something outside of ourselves, that we find meaning. All these connections lead to human moments. We hold these moments in our hearts long after they occur and feed on them when we are hungry for something to lift our spirits, the movement in our minds.

Let's look at the gestures in three films.

In *Garfield*, when he was told to go and chase a mouse, Garfield stands there with his paws pointing up and claws bent over and says, 'I don't do the digging thing.'

In the *Pacifier*, the younger girl is asked who messed up the Girl Guide stand. If she had been confident in her own self, she could have used her outstretched arm to show where the boys had gone. However, she just has her hands clenched in front of her and points with a finger without even taking her hand away from her body.

In the picture *Instinct* with Anthony Hopkins, where he is in prison, he finds the prisoners being manipulated by the guards and the bully. A pack of cards is dealt out to the prisoner, but the bully always gets the ace of hearts; this is the card which allows a prisoner to go out into the sunshine for half an hour. One day, on getting the card, Anthony Hopkins confidently holds his card out from his body and tears it in half. The prisoners look aghast. They think he is very brave but stupid. But then one of the other prisoners, not the bravest soul, with his hand near his chest had a bit of a grin on his face as he tears his card.

Movement enhances your story.

First story

The Dining Room Table

There were many tall stories, secrets, laughter, and raised voices that occurred around the dining room table. It stood powerful and strong, with solid wooden legs and a well-polished, shiny wooden surface. Before these dinners, it was my job to set the dining table. A lace cloth was used, and I made sure each corner had the same amount of crocheted edging over the edge. The butter plates were next then the silver cutlery, which I set down with a slight snap; a bowl of sugar cubes, which might have had one or two less in the bowl by the time I left the room; and a tiny crystal salt bowl with the smallest little spoon.

The dining table was only used when we had visitors, relatives, and friends—some noisy, some gentle, quiet people. The conversations could get quite rowdy. There were big discussions, sometimes heated discussions, carried on at the table. There could be raucous laughter and perhaps gossip sometimes.

But this was a very placid household, and when everyone had left, the table would be cleared, the cloth removed and put out in the laundry. The table was left standing alone in the dining room. It was as if the night's excitement was removed with the gathering of the plates and removal of the tablecloth. Silence would fall on everything except the mantel clock, which seemed to seize the moment and begin to tick louder, steadily ticking, insisting that time kept passing, anticipating its chiming on the hour. The household would return to its placid self, knowing neither grand excitement nor great sorrow.

Second Story

All She Needed to Know She Learned in the Garden

I could speak, I could hear, and I could see. I was in touch with reality. But today, my imagination was going to expand my thinking in a way that was like having a light shining on my reality, revealing it in a new way.

I was just a little girl, around about seven. I was in the kitchen. I took a biscuit and made a Vegemite sandwich, cutting it into quarters. I placed them in the centre of one of father's handkerchiefs. I went outside, and as the door slammed, my mother called out, 'Don't be long.' But I was hardly listening as I was too busy tying the ends of the handkerchief to the end of a stick. I had a vision of an adventure like the stories my mother had read to me.

Today I was going to be Dick Whittington. I placed the stick over my shoulder. My eyes had a twinkle in them, and a small smile played around my mouth. I wished my cat would follow me all the way, like Dick Whittington's cat, but I knew he wouldn't.

I marched across the backyard past the clothes line between the two lemon trees and through the opening in the back fence. Bertie, the cat, was following. I went past the peppercorn trees, past the brown 1932 Fiat truck. Some days it was stacked as high as can be, ready to go to market, but not this day. I walked and walked and walked along the dusty track, jumping the occasional puddle left from the recent rain.

I came to the rows of lettuces with leaves in many shades of gentle green. I stopped, spotting a ladybird on a lettuce leaf; I picked up the little red beetle with black spots on it and said, 'Ladybird ladybird fly away home, your house is on fire your children are burning.' The ladybird then flew away.

I was now 100 yards from home, but I hadn't reached my destination. I stopped and looked over a ploughed paddock on my left. My mind went back to the day not long ago when I was down here with my father. He was burning off rubbish, and I had left my teddy too close to the fire. He had been badly burnt; his face had been singed, and he had lost a foot in the tragic accident. I remember how I gave him a nice little burial, shedding a tear or two, as my teddy had been a special friend for as long as I could remember. I recalled also how I had raced back the next day. I wanted to dig him up because, burnt or not, I still wanted him, but when I got near the place, I could see the land had been ploughed, and it was impossible to know where I had buried him.

I then soberly walked on. There on my right was my favourite vegetable, the turnip. The leaves were a powerful green, and the roots were white and purple. I didn't like to eat them, but I thought they were so pretty and wondered how the common brown earth could produce something so beautiful.

I could see a man ahead of me, he was kneeling on one knee, leaning over and thinning out some small plants. He had a grey weather-beaten hat upon his head, his well-worn chequered shirt was faded from the sun, and his pants with patches on the knees were getting dirt on them as he worked with the earth. I thought he looked just about the most handsome man in the whole world. He was so intent in his work he had not heard me coming as he whistled while he worked. So I sat down among the carrots and wondered about the daily chores he had to do.

I'd seen him plough the soil in preparation for planting the seeds during this time, keeping the soil free from weeds so that when he planted when the time was right, the seeds would grow healthy.

I'd seen him walk up and down the furrows, up and down, up and down, scattering the seeds in the grooves he'd made on the top of the furrow. How did he have the patience to sow the seed like this?

He seemed quite ageless even though he had worked over the years in the pouring rain and the blazing sun. I sat there still with the stick with my lunch on the end draped over my shoulder. Then suddenly, I knew that he had to patiently wait for the right season for the right plants so the seedlings could take root in the prepared, weed-free, fertile soil. Each plant had its own particular need and time for growing. There was no use rushing and racing; in its own time, it would be ready.

I watched as he thinned the plants out. I did not understand why he was pulling out what seemed to me to be good plants. No, I did not understand that thinning out was necessary for the remaining shoots to grow bigger and stronger, but I did know that you just had to ride with the seasons with the help of watering and let nature take its course.

I may have thought that my thinking was just my imagination, but what was my imagination if not the place where I discovered and played with the truths of the universe?

I stood up, and little did I know that what I had learned that day was the way of life, even my own life, that the ordinary brown earth could grow beautiful vegetables, and that so too could beautiful things grow out of a plain, ordinary life.

I learned that life was about pain, preparation, patience, and getting rid of what will hinder good, healthy growth.

I approached the man and said, 'Hello, Daddy, I've come to have lunch with you.'

Adjectives: can make your story come alive
upending, refreshing, excited, creative, content, unusual, busy, rewarding, happy, frustrating

* * *

We are happy in our latter years, but can feel restless when our children and grandchildren throw their persistent *youth*, *vitality*, and *energy* across the memories of our mind.

Adjectives

Note how these adjectives help reinforce how you feel about a situation: *upending, refreshing, excited, unusual, happy, frustrating, busy, rewarding, creative, content.*

Rewarding

On walking into the staffroom, I heard a teacher talking about my course. I found it quite *rewarding*. It took place in a state school, I took grades 5 and 6 for a session of eight weeks of Public Speaking and Personal Development. The teacher was saying how good the course was, saying, 'As teachers, we teach them things they need to learn, but this course was teaching them how to live life.' Sometimes when people say nice things about us, we get really embarrassed, but I knew the perfect reaction, and that was to just say, 'Thank you.'

Upending

Nat's grandfather died, so Paul and Nat needed to go up to northern NSW for the funeral. This was upending as Paul, Nat, and Madison had to immediately get on the road, Tayla and Jayden had to pack a bag and come to stay with me, and I needed to make sure the courses and things I was doing during the week it was fitting in with their timetable.

Refreshing, Excited, Happy, Content

They settled into their usual rooms. They usually stayed in on Thursday nights. We all got on very well, which we usually did. It was *refreshing* having them come home from school, bursting in to tell me things that had happened during the day. I recalled how I would try to be home when my children were young, as when they got home was the only time they wanted to share the *excited* about the day. Half an hour later, they were past the news and on to something else. It was unusual to have them there for ten days, but everyone was *happy* and *content*.

First Story

Not a Perfect Life, Just Perfect Moments

Second Story

Not a Good Time in My Life

First Story

Not a Perfect Life, Just Perfect Moments

Dorothy Rowe tells a story in one of her books about a journalist, Martin Flanagan, being at a railway station. It's the story of a man giving his lunch to birds. This is the main external thing going on, but see the many thoughts and feelings that are going on inside his mind.

He says it is one of those moments of equilibrium to be found some morning between home and work. The train is still to arrive, the sun is shining, and two grey speakers above the platform are broadcasting Paul Simon's popular hit song: 'People say she's crazy. She wears diamonds on the soles of her shoes.' A fellow commuter has paused in his path and is burrowing into his lunch box. He produces an iced bun, which he throws on the platform on the other side of the track.

The rest of the commuters look up from books and newspapers and note his strange behaviour, but he is oblivious of the silent scrutiny. A sparrow lands next to the bun. The man continues to burrow and emerges with a sandwich, which he propels in the same direction.

Tomato splatters on the bitumen. It is altogether too human. One waits for a member of the metropolitan constabulary to appear from behind the bushes and effect an arrest. No one appears, just another sparrow, and the birds' benefactor trundles wordlessly on his way.

Paul Simon is clearly unperturbed because he keeps singing. The sun keeps shining, and the music merges with the moment.

The train finally arrives. The feast is being enjoyed by two pigeons, two mynah birds, and nine sparrows, and Martin's book lies defeated on his lap.

There aren't necessarily happy endings, just perfect moments.

* * *

Brett and I went to England to see my other son and family, and getting there, we spent a couple of days in Vienna, Austria. One day we had an early start on a bus trip to visit where *The Sound of Music* was made. We were sitting in the bus, too early for the hustle and bustle of crowds of people, when across the corner parkland, an elderly lady came. She walked to the middle of the park. All of a sudden, about fifty pigeons swooped down very close to her head. In the next moment, she opened a bag and threw seeds and bread for the birds. She folded the bag, put it in her pocket, and walked away. This all happened in a minute, and then she was gone; it was a magical moment.

Second Story

Not a Good Time

It was three minutes to midnight. A brilliant flash of lightning was followed by a very loud and rumbling clap of thunder, and rain pelted down on the roof. My house, along with the rest of the suburb, lost power. Four hours later, power was restored. It was inconvenient for everyone, but its effect on our household was enormous. In our house, it was a crisis, a life hung in the balance.

The tension in our household was fragile at this time. Two of my three boys were asthmatics. Brett was having a particularly bad time with his asthma, especially at night. It was common for me to be up two or three times a night to him. He was lucky if he could sleep for four hours without waking with a bad coughing attack. I would get up and put his pump on him as he was coughing too much to manage anything.

This night, it was ten past twelve. In the dark of the stormy night with a flickering candle on his desk, I tried to give him his Ventolin inhaler, but he was coughing out and out with just the tiniest breath in; he just couldn't get air or the Ventolin into his lungs. I told God in no uncertain terms that he was not having Brett too; John, his father, had died three weeks earlier from cancer, and now, three weeks later, which just happened to be John's birthday, Brett was fighting for each breath.

All of a sudden, he had a convulsion, which caused him to throw himself out of the bed. There he was lying on the floor, not breathing. I lifted his limp body to a sitting position and gave him mouth-to-mouth resuscitation; after five breaths, he gave a jump and started breathing. I brought the candle closer and was shocked to see the look on his face; he was staring at the ceiling with eyes that seemed to have no colour. The pupils had dilated and seemed to take up the whole iris.

After getting him back to bed, I went and took some cough medicine, which I knew had chloroform in it, and went back to bed. As my head lay on the pillow, I gave a big sigh, expecting it to relieve the tension of my tangible despair. It was no use taking him to the hospital; the crisis was over. Quite a few nights I had taken him to the hospital, but they just given me a pat on the hand, like I was some kind of idiot and said, 'Just give him the pump every four hours. He'll be all right.'

Who really cared about Brett? Brett was very shy and wouldn't talk to people he didn't really know. He was not overweight and looked normal, but he did have a disability. He couldn't read or write. He really thought like anyone else, but unfortunately, it was by his disability that people defined him.

In the morning, I didn't tell his brothers and sent them off to school. I was angry with the world. I didn't ring anyone to tell them. However, that day, a few people rang, and a few called in probably because they knew it was John's birthday.

What was I to say? I didn't want to talk about it, to anyone, I was angry. It was the only thing I did—avoiding saying something. Sometimes I hated words because they told the truth about things. Even a lie would let the truth sneak in. So when they said the usual 'How are you?' I knew the usual 'I'm fine' wouldn't cut it. I really didn't want to share my real feelings. I had a father, sister, brother, and many friends, but as we each grew, life had drawn us in different directions and different worlds. Although I was very close to them, their worlds were very different from mine, which made other people seem strangers. So I briefly told them with a sad little smile on my face, and I spoke without emotion or feeling.

One night the next week, I parked outside the children's hospital with Brett asleep on the back seat. Then sometime after midnight, he started coughing, and I decided to take him into the hospital. Then I was standing before the doctor, a medium-built man with a white coat, a stethoscope hanging around his neck. He had a look of 'If you have a problem, I can fix it'. I said, 'This is what I am trying to tell you is happening.'

Brett was admitted to the hospital and was fine the next day. When I thought about it, he was always fine the next day, which left me with a feeling of 'What am I doing wrong?' I asked a nurse about it, and she said, 'They gave him an injection of cortisone. It works very quickly.' Well, 'works very quickly' was true, but I also learned a week later that although it was very good for getting over the asthma attack, it was not good for the body. I was told that our own bodies could make cortisone, but when after massive doses by injection, the patient's body would say, 'Oh, lots of cortisone, I don't need to make any.' And so with his body not producing cortisone, he would be on this roller-coaster ride of being injected with and his naturally produced cortisone eventually depleting. His body would say 'Time for another asthma attack', and so he would get on the cycle again.

I eventually heard of a doctor in Wagga Wagga who had cured many asthmatics, so up there we went. On returning to Melbourne, Brett was all right for a few days, and we had two more trips to Wagga Wagga. This doctor apart, from other medications, gave him cortisone tablets. He started off with two, and it was weaned down every few days by a quarter of a tablet. Within a month, he was down to a quarter of this tiny tablet. 'By doing it this way,' the doctor had said, 'by the time you get near the end, Brett's own body will know it needs to make some to top up.' That was the end of our hospital visits, and Brett rarely had a bad asthma attack. If he did, it was because of some other underlying problems.

Life continued for us, like every family, with ups and downs. We'd win some battles, and we'd lose some. It didn't make it any easier to cope with problems, just made it more familiar. There were still days when the kids were ill or the dog would break off his chain or there'd be thrips on the washing. There were still days that were just a little above average but basically nothing good or bad. They were just different, less tortured.

And now, this part of my diary is getting filed away in a cupboard because I don't want to think about it.

A metaphor. **When you are telling a story, but it is really not the story that is really on you mind. Mine is about, what was happening when my sister went on the walk I really wanted to go on. But now instead of being angry, when I think of the occasion, I will think of the story, but I will really remember, why I was really there.**

* * *

Opportunities are usually disguised as hard work so most people don't recognise them.

The true art of memory is the art of attention.

Sometimes you just have to bow your head say a prayer and weather the storm.

First Story

Write about an event, something that happened but it was what you have not mentioned, which caused the memory

Second Story

Talk about a decision, that was not the best you've made or a situation where you're done something and said, 'What was I thinking?'

First Story

At Apollo Bay on a Saturday, we were a few minutes early to go to visit friends, so we stopped where we could park off the ocean road and walked on the sand. The waves were breaking, with fluffy foam caressing the shoreline. There was a large creek streaming into the sea. The water, before reaching the sea, was hurtling under a bridge, around rocks, then dropping to the sand before coming to the sea. Back up the creek, the water came to a place where it bumped into three rocks. Some water went between the two big rocks, and then water hit the other big rock that had been like in a triangle to the other two rocks. Some water sneaked through the gaps, but most of it swirled around in circles, not sure where to go.

The water that had gone to the left hit another big rock but found its way easily around it without other interruptions as it proceeded. The water to the right did some swirling too before it hit the strands of seaweed, but it too then proceeded without further interruption to the sea. The water along the edges flowed easily and gently along, away from the flurry in the centre.

We can be afraid of really getting into life, afraid it might hurt us; it may be too hard, or there are too many unexpected surprises. We can just go along the edges of life, where it is safe, but we'll miss out on a lot of learning experiences and a lot of excitement. Who wants to just sit and watch life go by? There is no life that is going to go along perfectly all the time. You're still going to bump into the side and get knocked around. So why not get into life and experience what it has to offer you?

Some of the water is swishing over one big rock as if to say anyone can do this. Are you even in the water or just sitting on the edge of the river of life, trying to see what you can get out of life without even getting wet? You have to actually dive in and be part of the river to really experience it. Feel the flow of the river, experience different parts of it. Get with the flow, and really experience it. It may carry you to new adventures. Life is forever changing. A river has many phases as life does. When it is sunny, it looks fast and exciting, but when it is cold and raining, it looks angry and wild. But that's life, forever changing.

Make the most of it because the creeks is just about to come to the end of its individual existence; it is about to enter the ocean. The ocean will swallow the creek up in its powerful waves and tides and undertows, and it will never again make its own decisions. It will be part of the powerful sea, and it may forget it ever had a life of its own. So live life while you can learn and discover, and make the most of it.

So this is what you call a metaphor. A story symbolising something else.

As for me, I was with my sister later that afternoon. I had wanted to go on this river search, but she had wanted to walk up to a lookout first, and I didn't have the energy to walk any further, partly because I had arthritis in my right knee. So I sat on a rock while she went on a two-kilometre walk. I sat on the rock, looking at the river, so whenever I read this story, I would know exactly where I was and why I was there. I would also remember that I was sitting on a rock by a river, which was also the edge of a cow paddock. I had really wanted to do this walk and was a bit cross with my sister that we hadn't done it first.

When she came back, raving about how beautiful it was, she said, 'Why are you sitting here where it's so smelly?'

I replied, 'It wasn't smelly before you came here. You just walked through cow poop. Karma maybe?'

Second Story

Karate

Have you ever been to a karate class? I had an ever-so-nice, gentle-looking lady come to my door, inviting me to go to a karate class.

The thought of going to a karate class had never crossed my mind before, but Brett, my son, was home this night, so I invited her in. Brett has always had a hankering to do karate. He taught himself t'ai chi from a videotape. He seemed to have a bit of a talent for rhythm. Quite a few years before, Brett and I had gone up to Darwin to see a friend of mine. It just happened that the week we went up there was National Fitness Week, which my friend Liz was really into. As for me, well, I'm not really into such things. All these five-kilometre walks are not really my thing. And it didn't help that, in the last agonising kilometre, there was this little kid who had done the walk with his family, running and leaping all over the place. There was one morning we got up really early to do t'ai chi on the beach. Liz and I were fumbling along with the routine. When we arrived back in Melbourne a week later, the whole thing was a complete blur to me, but Brett could still remember a lot of the routine.

So that was why I thought karate would be good for Brett, and this lady convinced me that, seeing I was going to take Brett, I might as well join too. It did sound rather logical. And good intentions die unless they are executed. But the alarms bells should have rung because as I told you, I'm not into exercise. So we were all set for Sunday—Brett rather excited, me apprehensive. The only aspect of it that calmed the spirit within me was that it was non-contact karate.

Sunday came, and karate was quite an ordeal. I found muscles I never knew I had. I was tired, and my coordination definitely left something to be desired. I was labouring to do things I usually did on autopilot. This was because at no time did both my arms go in the same direction, and not only that—if one fist was facing up, the other was either facing down or sideways. Within half an hour, I was seriously wondering whether this class went for one hour or for one and a half. I'd just die if it went for two hours. I looked around, and most looked happy to be there, but I was there in body, not spirit. I was trying to remain positive, knowing that being negative would drag me down mentally, emotionally, and physically. One hour came and went. I was looking out of the window, at the houses over the road, envying the people sitting comfortably and watching TV. Maybe their coordination wasn't any better than mine, but they didn't know it. And I also would be happy not to know it. Ignorance is bliss. I was too old for this. After an hour and a half, we were released from the building, and we headed straight for the supermarket to get something to eat.

As I was driving along, thinking how stupid I was for going to the class, the sun was shining brightly. The weather that day had been very strange. It would rain, pouring for fifteen minutes, and then the sun would come out for fifteen minutes, but you could see the next wave of black clouds rolling in. After choosing what we wanted, we went through the checkout. By this time, it was pouring raining again, and just to make idle conversation I said, 'It was warm and sunny fifteen minutes ago.' Owing to her reply, she must have completely missed seeing it as she rolled her eyes and said, 'I always get these delusional people come through my checkout.'

I looked at my watch. It was only lunchtime, and so far today, I was stupid and delusional. If this was the first day to the rest of my life, I was in trouble. Later that afternoon, I did a lot of ironing and had to admit that it was better than karate. By late afternoon I had a Bacardi and Coke, that was definitely better then karate. I was even weighing up if a visit to the dentist was equal to it.

By nightfall, my spine felt that it had stretched in ways that had been long forgotten. My calf muscles were letting me know where they were, and my bed—oh, my bed—was looking very good.

The next day, I felt OK. I went off to work, and I was rather quiet. I didn't say a word about karate. I just quietly worked away and left the others to talk. After a couple of hours, it was noticed that I was quiet, and they came to the conclusion that I was quiet because I had been up to something during the weekend. How could I tell them? Eventually, I did because they were guessing what they thought I had been up to, which was much more wondrous and exciting, so I told them. I told them everything, every detail.

I told them and illustrated how we swung our arms, our really fast—ow. I wish I hadn't done that. I found there were muscles in my forearms and elbows that were objecting to strenuous movement today. I showed them how we had to kick—ow. I wished I hadn't done that too. Did you know that it could hurt right down the thigh bone, in your hips, your calf muscles, and even in the arch of your foot? After this, I didn't give them any more demonstrations because I felt OK as long as I didn't do anything. I was going to go back, but I didn't. I decided I'd rather do the ironing.

Enthusiasm, where you were stirred, motivated, eager to meet the challenge.

Sometimes it's easier to go back to the original concept rather than design further thinking. NASA found that pens wouldn't write in space without gravity, so they eventually designed a space pen with a forced ink system. However, when the Russians came across the same problem, they thought back to the concept of writing and using a pencil.

But it turned out the Americans did have the right idea as when the Russians broke a tip off the pencil, that bit would float around and could be very dangerous.

***

Sometimes enthusiasm is appreciated, and sometimes it isn't. One of the jobs I had later in life was in a warehouse a few days a week. I had to go up to the front of the building first thing and tell the guys who filled the orders what I needed. Every day I had to go with the same request. It would save me time if it was already there; they did know what I needed. I cured them with my enthusiasm. I would go up to them and say, 'Good morning, everyone. Isn't it a lovely day?' Then Dale or Dean, who either hadn't had enough sleep or just weren't awake yet, would look at each other and say, 'Who's going to bash her, you or me?' So they found the mornings easier to cope with by having what I wanted waiting there for me.

We are always eager to get to our destination when we have a plan, but in actual fact, the journey getting there can be more intriguing than the destination.

I heard a man tell a story one day. His plane landed at Singapore, but he hadn't booked ahead to stay at a hotel. He saw a man standing, holding a sign which said, 'The Hyatt Hotel.' Chris thought, *Hmm, yes, that's where I would like to stay.* So he went up to the man holding the sign and said, 'I'm going to the Hyatt.' The man looked down his list of names. Now it would have been a complete miracle if his name was there because he hadn't booked. The man, having looked down his list, said, 'I'm sorry, sir. Your name doesn't seem to be on my list, and my car will be full. Would it be all right if I called a taxi for you?' Chris said that would be nice. On arriving at the hotel, the doorman stepped forward opened the door and said, 'Welcome to the Hyatt. May I get your baggage?'

Now compare this to when I arrived in Australia. I did the same thing. I went up to the man holding the Hyatt sign and said I was staying at the Hyatt. He looked down his list, and my name wasn't there, so he said, 'Your name's not on the list. Sorry, mate, there's no more room in the car. If you just go over there, you'll find a taxi rank.'

First Story

Have you ever treated someone with dignity and respect and been surprised at the results

Second Story

Unwelcomed guests, or something you went whole heartedly at, to achieve you're goal.

First Story

Treating Someone with Respect

Have you ever treated someone with dignity and respect and been surprised at the result?

One school I was teaching in was in a real working-class area, and some of the classes left something to be desired. In one class, there was a boy who was most disruptive (we are talking about grade 6 students, not little children). He would interrupt whenever he felt like it even though the teacher was in the room. In the course I ran, the students were asked to do three speeches over the term. Each speech was to be up to three minutes long. Let's call him Mark. Mark did his speeches, but his thoughts were all over the place. He was more interested in entertaining the class with his antics. He really did have the gift of the gab.

On Mark's last speech, I commented, 'When you grow up, the perfect job for you would be to be a car salesman because you've got personality and the gift of the gab. But if you are selling a car, you have to stay on the subject. You're one aim should be to sell a car. At the moment, in your speeches, you are changing the subject and not sticking to what you are meant to be talking about.' After the lesson, he came up to me and asked if he could do his last speech again next week. The following week, he spoke, sticking to the subject. He was pleased with himself.

I was pleased with him. The teacher was amazed, and the class was jubilant.

Some people just need to know that someone is expecting something from them and knows that they can do it. We shouldn't forget that the mind of a child can be like a far country and sometimes impossible to explore.

Second Story

Unwelcome Guests

They could be heard but not seen because they came and left at night. We could hear them moving in the ceiling. That was in between my bedroom and Brett's bedroom upstairs. There were possums in the ceiling. Now if they had been quiet, we may never have known they were there, but it must have been mating season, for there was a lot of commotion going on. How they were getting in was a mystery to me. I had to wait till dark when they were leaving to find the small hole they were entering the house by. Something had to be done about it.

I tried to get Brett to block off the hole by climbing out on the roof, but he was not keen on upsetting the little critters, so I waited a couple more weeks until Brett had had enough of being woken at 5.30 a.m., which was when they came in. We put plan number 1 into action. We stuffed three long pieces of wood up the hole. The next morning, on their arrival, they were not happy about this and let us know, so I raced up the stairs and thought I'd make a lot of noise by racing across the balcony to scare them away. But on getting to the glass door to the balcony, right in front of me was the cutest little possum just looking at me.

When I pulled myself together to get on with my ruthless plan, it ran away when I opened the door. Thank goodness. I raced out, making a lot of noise. They were supposed to be frightened and run away and never come back again, but they merely moved a bit further along the roof and looked at me. I eventually tired of this game at 5.30 in the morning. I went back to bed, defeated, and then they proceeded to pull each of the pieces of wood out, which of course made loud, crashing noises as each piece hit the concrete ground.

The next day, I climbed the ladder to survey the situation for myself and put plan number 2 into action, again striking after dark. I waited till 9.30, which was the time they usually were out. I went out, climbed the ladder armed with wood, gloves, torch, and chicken wire; the chicken wire was rolled up really tightly. I could see the bushy-tailed possum on the garage roof. I shoved the wire up the hole and then the pieces of wood to really jam it in. Then I pushed the lead or whatever—the soft metal—under the edge of the tile, and I secured the tiles and thought, *They will never get in now.*

Let me tell you something about plan number 2. You must always—I mean, always—make sure they're all out. This little problem I had not foreseen. On being in my bedroom a little later, I could hear noises in the ceiling. There was a great commotion going on. The one on the inside wanted to get out, and the ones on the outside were trying to get in; it was not a calm situation. It was now 10 p.m. I said to Brett, 'It's too late to do anything about it tonight.' Brett and I went to the other end of the house and watched TV, trying to ignore the whole situation. By twelve o'clock, they had pulled out all the wood and wire and had left.

On their return at 5 a.m. the next morning, I had a couple of buckets of water. I planned to throw the water over them. They would have their feelings so hurt that they wouldn't come back again. With all my might, I threw the water. I don't think a drop got on them. They merely stepped sideways, but the gusty wind did manage to blow a fair proportion of it back at me. You can see I was not having a great deal of success, but I was not giving up as this process has consumed me.

Now the neighbours were probably setting their alarm clocks for 5.30 just to see what this crazy lady next door would do next. I hope you're not getting tired of this story, but it was the most exciting thing that had been happening in my life for quite a few months. These possums have turned me into a fearsome and eccentric woman racing across the balcony in my nightie in the dead of night.

That night, I sat in Brett's bedroom and waited. At 9.30, one left. Twenty minutes later, a mother and baby left, and a bit later, another left. Off I went with plan number 3. I had a feeling of courage (fear that has said its prayers). I climbed up the ladder again. I hate ladders; ladders to me are like having a very slippery grip on life. In the dark of night, I was armed with a carefully cut-out piece of wood to fit the offending hole and polyfilla and a hammer and nails. With each step up the ladder, my anger and determination was mounting.

There was a lot of manoeuvring going on there in the darkness of the moonlit night. Loud banging echoed sharp and clear, shattering the silence of the night. I nailed the fascia board back in place and then fitted the carefully shaped piece of wood over the offending hole and, finally, squeezed the poly filler into any space I could see. My breath halted, and my brows were hot with determination and concentration. I descended from the ladder and triumphantly returned inside, feeling invincible. I did not feel unjustified in my actions. Whose house was this? They didn't pay for it.

They came back every morning for a week, making terrible noises, trying to get in. I mean, I can understand it's not easy finding accommodation for four. About six months later, I put the house up for sale. I thought I had better clean the garage door; it was a big roll-up door which I rarely used. If the possums had been living in the garage, I didn't care. On pulling down the door, I heard a rumbling noise, and a possum nearly fell out. That must have been their home. Oh dear, I forgot to tell the people who bought the house.

Verbs

'Sit table'- is not a sentence. 'Sit at this table'- is a sentence

Verbs also tell tenses, (present) I move, (past) I moved, (Future) I will move, (Condition) If I moved it,

My son was explaining to hi nan who'd just had her ninetieth birthday, the advantages of long-term savings plans. She smiled as said, "Son, at my age, I think twice before buying green bananas.

First Story

True Heroes of the World Do Good and then Disappear Or who has been a hero in your life?

Second Story

I'll, never ever do that again. Or a time you were braver than you intended to be

First Story

True Heroes of the World Do Good and Then Disappear.

The majority of parents I know fulfil the essential definition of a hero, which is someone who acts selflessly in favour of something beyond themselves. It is an act of will rather than some passive ability. It is listening to the inner voice and acting upon it. World leaders and famous people might be monuments of greatness, but parents are living embodiments of unconditional love, service, and dedication. No other people actually do more to make the world a better place for someone else. Parents are the *grass roots* of humanity.

Few parents realise that offspring that turn out to be good citizens are something they have created; they don't just fall out of the sky.

Frances was a hero in our lives. We met her through Brett after he had his eyes tested to see if he was dyslectic. He didn't quite fit into the normal dyslectic sphere, but he fell into it sometimes. We became friends. She invited us to her place, and the three of us would play games of Yatzy on the computer many afternoons. She knew Brett was more capable then he was letting on, so we did things that did not look like work to him but stimulated his mind. Frances was a retired headmistress. She moved here from England after retiring and, having never been married, did not have an abundant amount of friends, only those she met through working. This included us.

This was when I still had all my boys living at home. It was a hectic time in my life, probably about six years after my husband had passed, a time when my self-esteem was more centred on survival than achieving anything for myself. This was around the time I nervously joined Toastmasters, a public-speaking organisation. Though it was not bringing more pleasure than pain to my already stretched mind, it did take my mind into another direction. Frances encouraged me, and we talked a lot and talked in a way that I did not do with anyone else. Her words reached inside me and touched my heart. Her eyes radiated intelligence and a fiercely independent point of view. We talked about achieving things and wonderful things we learned in books.

I'd grown up in a placid home, and the feelings were more about me existing and being happy but not about achieving. I did not realise it at the time, but she kept expressing how I was going to really grow through this Toastmasters experience, which I surely did. Before her passing, she had said I would be doing something like I am today—teaching in schools and sessions like this. This was years before it happened, but she sowed the seed that grew within me.

Frances is one of the heroes that came into my life, made a difference, and left. On her passing, I was reflecting what she had meant to Brett and I. I thought she had been there to help Brett advance, but she did as much and more for me. I learned to more than exist but reach for the stars. She was a rare person—not only older, but wiser.

Second Story

Holidaying in Myrtleford, I'll Never, Ever do that Again

Everybody needs a holiday, but could the three young boys and I do a camping trip on our own? I mean, camping was good, but could I pull a trailer? That would be a new experience. Backing it—well, that wouldn't be necessary. I was going straight to Myrtleford. My eldest son, who was thirteen, assured me backing was easy. I was hoping that my brother and his family would have already arrived up there and would back the trailer for me. After successfully manoeuvring the windy road up to Alexander, I forged on with undying confidence that I could do it. We stopped at Benalla for lunch after successfully finding a car space that I could just pull into. Almost reaching Myrtleford, I was pulled up by the police and informed that my left blinker light on the trailer wasn't working. He let me proceed after I promised to have it fixed on our arrival at our destination.

Exhausted after hours of driving, there was the putting-up of the tent to do before relaxation could be thought about. The tent—well, let's just say tempers were flaring by the time the last peg went in.

Many days were beginning warm, with cotton clouds in the blue sky, and the heat grew as the day progressed. We wondered how we could be complaining about the cold nights when it was so hot during the day. But there we were, not five hours later, huddled around the open campfire, absorbing the heat. We listened to the crackle of flames as they devoured the dry wood, sending determined threads of smoke into the sky. Sparkles flew as a log collapsed in the fire. Some nights when there was a little rain, the angry fire spat, sizzled, and hissed as if enraged by the light rain.

But there was only so long that young boys could sit still and enjoy the leaping flames. They said, 'Let's go and play a game.' So we went back to our tent. There in the light of a flickering lantern, we sat around the card table. We began throwing the dice for snakes and ladders. I was sitting there with three professional snakes-and-ladders players all under the age of thirteen. We were eating potato chips and betting with Smarties. I seemed to be the only one landing on snakes and the only one playing around the bottom of the board. I was sure they were cheating at every chance they got, but I couldn't prove it.

A few moths were flying around the lantern at great speed. Every once in a while, one would hit the hot glass and go *pss* and spin out of control and crash and go plummeting to the ground. Suddenly, one shot up into the air and landed in a spider web, where the spider came along, wrapped it securely in more of its web, left it there to dine on later, and then crawled back along its web to wait for the next moth. We sat there with our mouths ajar, spellbound by the ruthless, single-minded efficiency of the spider.

We looked at one another, and this broke the spell cast over us. The boys, recovering and encouraged by this homicidal scene, started running around, arms flailing, trying to get more moths to go into the spider's web. That was the end of snakes and ladders. I left the table, telling them I wouldn't play with mercenaries, and they replied that they wouldn't play with someone who ate all the potato chips. I went to bed thinking, *If our future is in the hands of fickle minds like these, we're in trouble.*

Every day I went for a swim. I swam as fast as I could against the current, but the current was so strong that I didn't really move. The Ovens River swiftly turned corners like it was on a mission, refusing to be slowed by rocks or turns.

Holidays are great, but invariably, there is a 'I'll never, never do that again', and this holiday was no exception. Apart from being very fast-flowing, the river was also deep in places and very cold. In all, there were about ten kids in our small camping group, and they thought the fast-flowing river was great. Some would go 100 metres up the river, come hurtling down on their lilos, slip off at a shallow spot, and wade to the edge. I watched this for many days, lots of laughter and fun.

I saw a couple of adults do it, so maybe I could. Gone was my usual sensible thoughts to myself, like '*Self, always be safe and careful.*' Did I mention *careful*? And that was how the idea just developed a momentum of its own. I'm not a courageous person, but what is courage if not foolhardiness bordering on stupidity?

I proceeded wearily up to where they entered the water. The embankment was steep. Within four steps, the water was up to my neck. Managing to get on to the lilo, which was a slippery critter, I thought I would go along the edge where the water was not moving so fast. But the lilo had a mind of its own, and the current pulled me out into the very life of the vast and moody river. Half a dozen of the kids went past, laughing with glee as they hurtled down the river.

I smiled at them, trying to have an air of confidence, poise, and balance. I had already made a mental note never to do this again. I was then out in a very fast bit of the river, and the turbulence was enough to unbalance me. I had no idea how to overcome this situation as thoughts were racing through my mind in chaotic disorder. One possible reason why things weren't going according to plan was that there never was a plan.

I fell off, thinking, *I'm going to drown*, but there I was, sitting in half a metre of water. That was why it was so fast because, in that spot, it was *shallow*. There was still another bend in the river before being in view of the tent dwellers, so nobody had seen this catastrophe. So suffering only personal humiliation (and today, I was going to ignore all atrocities except those that would break the skin), I continued down the river, and there, right in the middle of the river, was a dead tree stump—which, of course, my lilo was heading straight for.

I clung to the sides of the lilo so much that the blood drained from my knuckles. Somewhere tucked away in the corner of my mind was the information that I had to paddle to avoid this situation, but my hands couldn't seem to let go of the sides of the lilo. My heart was beating too fast. Rating was one part exhilaration, nine parts fear; the ratio was not good. I crashed gracelessly into the stump, and off I went again. The kids had never mentioned hitting the tree stump. I managed to disentangle myself and took a few deep breaths.

I was back on my lilo in a flash. Although my confidence was shattered, I glided around the corner, where I came into view of the campers. I tried to give a look of accomplishment, sophistication, and poise as I glided past them. On getting to my campsite, once again out of view of the other campers, I slid off the lilo, staggered to the embankment, clawed my way up to the top, kissed the grass, hugged a tree, sat confidently on a rock, leaned back, and smiled at the blue sky.

A neighbouring tent dweller came to speak to me. She said, 'That looked so exciting.'

I replied, 'I will never, never, never do that again.'

She talked for a couple of minutes and then said, 'Next time you do that, I'll come with you.'

I looked into her eyes, which appeared to be two blank discs, and I wondered which *never* she had not understood.

Emphasising emotion a need to explain the invisible

Pitch – 'What did you say' can be just a question, but if you want it to sound like a statement demanding an explanation, it come from deeper from down in the diaphragm.

Tone – sadness, happiness and boring all bring out different, tones of voice. This adds power to your story

Movement and tone, if you were to say 'come here' holding your hand out facing up and moving your index finger backward and forward, it is in forcing you statement. However if you were the hold your hand up and quickly move all your fingers toward you, it has become a more serious statement. But if you were to make the statement, with your hand out, palm down and index finger pointing down, it has become a much sterner statement.

First Story

Fear: Cause and Effect

Second Story

And the Pendulum Swings

> I was a make-up artist. A lady was forever saying to me that if I tried harder, I could make her look better. One day, she said, 'I feel beautiful.' This was the magic word: *feel*. She allowed herself to feel enthusiasm for herself, placing no restriction on her age. (Gregory Landsman)

First Story

Fear: Cause and Effect

Fear blocks our thinking, keeps us from trying, eats away at our self-esteem, stops us from reaching our goals. Then it has won.

I had a twig from a fuchsia tree hitting my bedroom window. My instant thought was, *You have to go. I don't need twigs hitting my window in the night and waking me.* But it was actually caused by a bird getting nectar from the flowers. I wonder how often we instantly think something is wrong when it is just something different, that something must be altered when it was just an instant of change and then going back to the original way.

Take, for example, this poem:

> Things that go 'bump' in the night
> Should not really give us a fright
> It's the hole in the ear
> That lets in the fear
> That and the absence of light.

One night, in the middle of the night, there was a loud bang. It woke me. I lay there in the dark, shaken from a sound sleep. My heart was thumping faster than normal. The noise had come from the en-suite.

I lay there, mind racing. What could I do? Did I really want to know at this hour? I looked at the dog, and the dog looked at me. We both decided that nothing could be done about it in the dead of a cold, dark, and a-little-bit-scary night, so we both went back to sleep. I must admit this gave me serious doubts as to the benefits of having a dog—you know, brave and protective under all circumstances!

In the morning, I found that the fan in the bathroom above the shower had fallen to the base of the shower.

Fear short-circuits our power. It removes our focus from everything else. It fills our minds, and it is the cause and effect.

A man wrote, 'The car alarm went off. I got such a fright. I almost did a commando roll to behind the rubbish bin.'

Fear itself isn't a weakness. The weakness is not admitting it but in keeping it inside for too long. Fear thrives in a dark place. You need to share it, drag it out into the open, and face it. Then it starts to shrink. Feelings can be like a wild animal. We underrate how fierce they are until we've opened their cages.

A class member (Barbara from Salford Parks) wrote, 'It was a beautiful, starry night, with a liquid moon shining in the sky. We had friends over for dinner. My twenty-one-month-old son, who didn't really believe in sleep, a frisky little fellow, was still up. I had my back to the balcony as we sat at the table; however, I could see the horrified looks on the faces of the people opposite me. I turned around, and there was my little son in his nightshirt standing on the railing of the balcony. We were five storeys up. He was pointing up, saying, "Look, stars." My husband was paralysed with indecision. I quietly arose and, gliding out to the balcony, said to my son, "Where are the stars?" He pointed up, showing me, and I slid my arms around him and took him inside.'

Someone said, 'The biggest roadblocks we encounter in life are the ones we construct ourselves.'

Second Story

And the Pendulum Swings

Things that we think are good may not be. Remember the story of Pandora's box? It was given to Pandora by Zeus with explicit instructions that it *was never to be opened*.

Well, she took it away with her on her honeymoon, and with it being a pretty dull honeymoon, she decided to open it. *Whoosh*. All the evils of the world escaped from the box. Illnesses of the body and sorrows of the minds. **Oops.** She knew what Zeus would say, 'Not happy, Pandora.'

She looked into the box; there was one thing left in there. Some say it remained in the box, others say it got out, but all agree that it was the last evil in the box. The last evil was *hope*. Most people would consider this good news. Did you ever consider hope as one of the evils of the world?

There are often events that happen that could have improved if we'd done more than hope, and the situation could have been better. But we just remained there passively, lethargically, hoping someone would help.

Is hope good or bad? The Pendulum swings.

I'll give you an example of where fear and hope got mingled together. Remember the story of when Brett, I and another boy were on the property at Warrigal, out in the middle of nowhere.

I returned to the cabin five minutes before Brett as he had stopped to talk to the horses. There were five horses in a paddock that we passed—one was a draught horse which Brett thought was so beautiful. But it didn't matter which angle I looked at it; I couldn't see that it outshone the others.

Where I had opened the cabin and then went outside again to put my towel out to dry. *Bang.* The door blew shut. It was 4 p.m. The shadows from the trees were growing fast as too was the fear inside me. The car keys were inside. *Somebody's got to help me.*

Then Brett had just arrived back from the dam. The thought that Brett could fit through that small window. And that was when hope changed from bad to good. What happened was what will always change hope from bad to good.

It was *action*. Hope needs action to make it positive.

It was *action* that made the pendulum swing.

Life is an interesting journey. So do you think that I have a balanced wholeness, me-ness? Not a chance. I'm a walking, talking paradox.

I'm shy, and I'm aggressive within the same body.

I'm lazy, and I'm hard-working.

I sometimes feel like giving up, but my spirit won't.

I get tired, but my spirit flies.

I feel tied down, but my spirit's free.

Hey, what the spirit is, I can be.

And the pendulum swings.

<u>Tell a story, tempo, excitement or boredom, I have used a repetitive phrase in the second story.</u>

First Story

Wanting to be the 'Centre of Attention'

Second Story

Write about an experience where you said, 'I didn't want to do it, but to keep her happy, I did it.'

* * *

> I would be unstoppable, if only I could get started
>
> I am a writer I give the truth scope.

First Story

The Centre of Attention

My parents were real actors, though not on the screen. When we had guests, my father, to become the centre of attention, would usually do it with his pipe. His chair would become a stage and his friends or family his audience. He'd crook one leg over the other, pick up pipe and knock it against the heel of his shoe, as though he was bringing a meeting to order. A tiny hunk of ash would spill from the bowl of his pipe into the carpet beneath him.

The roomful of people would by now be uneasily watchful. Then he'd sigh deeply, uncrook his leg, grunt a little and proceed to bend over to determine what to do with the ash. This was the master attention-getter. It never occurred to anyone watching, to go to his rescue. Usually Dad picked up the ash with the matchbox cover. However, in mid-bend, out of the corner of his eye, he would spot a piece of lint on the shoulder of his jacket. With the pipe in one hand, matchbox in the other, the focus of attention on the ash, he would slowly but surely proceed to flick any discernible flecks of lint he would find while everyone in the room waited on the fate of the ashes. His complete capture of attention accomplished, he was a happy man.

Mother would usually get up and go to the bathroom, returning after she sensed that Dad's act had run its course, she would then suggest a nice hot piece of apple pie that she had baked herself. In her striding toward the kitchen maybe she'd bump into a piece of furniture which would produce a startled gesture of sympathy from whoever was closest. . . . Mother had successfully stolen his thunder, Dad would proceed to get drunk, Mother was showing that every play must have more than one actor. (Shirley MacLaine, *Out on a Limb*)

* * *

Children easily become the centre of attention. On a Sunday, my son Paul and his family were over. Jayden was up on the roof, cleaning the spout along the veranda, as he was the only one light enough to walk on the tiles without breaking any. Tayla was helping me pull weeds out of the lawn, and Madison, who would be three next month, was picking up little bugs from the earth where Tayla was working.

Madison came and showed me a bug and said it was a boy bug.

I said, 'It's not a ladybird bug?'

She said, 'No it's a boy bug.'

Later, she showed me she had a worm in each hand, and a short time later, she came, looking sad, and said, 'I broke it.'

I said, 'What did you break?'

She said, 'The worm.'

Children become the centre of attention through innocence, whereas adults often plan a theatrical occurrence.

Second Story

Don't Tell Elaine

My sister and I go on regular holidays together, which is often quite stressful to me as there is one of us who likes to walk and one of us who doesn't. I'd rather do the ironing. I'm not really against walking. I mean, I've been doing it all my life.

We went to South Mole Island for our holiday; I think islands are for relaxing, sitting under the palm trees, surveying the scenery, feeling the sand between your toes, listening to the waves break on the shore, and watching the sunsets.

We walked every day. We became known to the fellow guests as the one who likes to walk and the one who doesn't. We had walked over all the flat areas, been on paddle-boards, swam, and even snorkelled in the ocean. Our second day on the island, we had climbed up and over one big hill, where a sign informed us it was one kilometre to the other side. It was so steep in one place near the top that they had constructed steps so holidaymakers wouldn't fall. Once on the other side, we went over a sandy beach then around a very tiny island, where we stumbled on pebbles, climbed over rocks, walked through knee-deep water in our effort to go completely around the island. Then, of course, we had to go back over the one-kilometre hill.

Still Elaine's energy level surged on, and I knew—I just knew—she would want to climb the mountain.

The next morning, I awoke to the loud ticking of the clock on the wall. I didn't stir, and I didn't want to wake Elaine. But I needn't have worried about that; she was already up. Then I smelt the coffee on the table, waiting for me. 'Coffee's ready,' she informed me brightly. I pulled the sheet over my head, wondering how someone could be so chirpy first thing in the morning. I arose with as much enthusiasm as I could muster. 'It's going to be a lovely day for walking,' she informed me. 'The sky is blue, the sea is green, and oh, here are your walking shoes.'

There she stood in shorts, walking shoes, a bright-red top, and her blond hair bounced as she walked towards me. I really did my best effort of bouncing out of bed with low-key enthusiasm. After breakfast, we set off.

My heart wasn't in it right from the start. Admittedly, they did have signs everywhere saying how far everything was. After we had gone the first kilometre, a sign we passed said, 'Two and a half kilometres to Menzies Point.' Now I didn't mean to be picky, but a quick calculation told me that two and a half plus the one we'd done made that three and a half, and by the time we got back, it would be seven kilometres.

Let me tell you about mountain climbing on tropical islands. There are no made footpaths, no handrails, and there are narrow tracks along the side of the mountain and a rocky path that needs to be watched. A foot in the wrong place could send you slipping over the edge or twisting an ankle. This means there is little time to really appreciate the scenery.

But we could hardly miss all the bats hanging in the trees just metres from where we were walking. I really would rather do the ironing. When we got to the top, the view was good—not great, just good. There was a seat at the top. Personally, I thought a drinking fountain would have been better, maybe a bar!

On our way back, I just knew Elaine was going to see the turn-off to Oyster Bay. On our way up, I had noted how steep the climb down was even though it was only one kilometre. I knew she'd want to go down there. I just knew it.

No matter how I distracted Elaine with 'Oh look, the walkway over to the island is underwater' or 'Oh, isn't that a lovely cloud up there?' or 'Oh, look at that island over there', we went down to Oyster Bay and back. I would like to stress again that I was not being picky, but that now made it nine kilometres by the time we got back.

When we got back to the resort, I wasn't backward in letting people know what my sister had made me do. Yes, I told them. Getting back to the room, I collapsed into a chair, and my head slumped on to the table, my arms sending papers floating to the floor. I felt like sliding on to the floor also and lying among the papers. But I thought that might be a bit melodramatic, and I did not want to betray to Elaine how unfit I was, though I really didn't feel as bad as I thought I would.

The next day, we played tennis. Now this didn't bother me as I knew I was the better tennis player. I was ready to have her running all over the court, but two games into the first set, Elaine lunged for the ball and felt something snap in her leg. She had pulled a tendon, collapsing on to the court. I went for help, and a nurse came with a wheelchair and wheeled her back to the first-aid room. She was so embarrassed to been seen like that.

That evening, when we went to dinner, Elaine was on crutches. She wanted to sit outside by the pool. I went inside to get our meals, which took a while. On returning to Elaine, I found it was raining, so I said, 'Why are you sitting in the rain?' Elaine replied, 'I didn't want anyone to see I had crutches.'

Elaine spent her last couple of days on the island on crutches. Poor Elaine, she couldn't walk. The last day I thought I'd be kind to her by doing the things she would like me to do. So I paddled out to see the coral for the last time. I walked the kilometre to the next bay. I mean, what's a kilometre? That afternoon, I did eight laps in the pool.

I'd say I was feeling fit, but *don't tell Elaine.*

Lateral thinking

In the story of when I went to have lunch with my father in the market garden, I explained, what he was doing, what he was wearing, and what I thought about the situation. Like lateral thinking, you can do it with a person or a scene, I prefer to do it on something specific, I find when reading a book, if they use lateral thinking on every situation, I get a bit tired of it and think, just get on with the story.

Who were your Parents, Aunt, or Anyone

How does she spend her day? Who is she really? I wonder what she was like when she was growing up. Did she get married, or was she alone, did she have children, or perhaps an animal. She has so many creases on her face, did they come from hardship? did those line around her eyes come from lots of laughter? Did she have the opportunity of making choices, did she have dreams she pursued, did she feel like a complete fulfilled person

First Story

The Worth of Money Changes Even People

Second Story

Talk about things that calm your mind and soul

* * *

Power can be misunderstood aggression, however it is confidence and stillness that is real power in ourselves, and acceptance. It takes effort to get a balance. The external world will jostle us around, but stillness can be stabilizing.

First Story

Can You Take the Value Away from Money or Your Own Life?

A lecturer asked, 'Who would like $20?' Several hands went up. He then screwed the $20 to a ball and asked again. Again several hands went up. This time, he screwed it up and dropped it on the floor and stood on it. Again he asked. He said, 'It doesn't matter what I do to this $20 note. It is still worth $20. So often in our lives, we are crumpled, trampled, ill-treated, insulted, yet despite all that, we are still worth the same.'

No matter how much help you may have received, you took that first breath by yourself and the next breath, and we take our last breath alone. No one will ever think one thought that is ours. No one will ever stand in our bodies, experience what happens to us, feel our fears, dream our dreams, or cry our tears. We are born, live, and leave this life entirely on our own. It is our responsibility. With positive actions and daily self-talk, you are consciously in charge.

Was there ever a time when your life seemed as though someone or life had treated you as though you had lost your worth?

When my husband was ill, two of my boys had asthma, and at times, the other one made my life seem like ten years of hard labour. There were many times I doubted my worth. Nothing I did helped to improve any one of their health problems. Of course, I was not really fully comprehending at the time that the boys' asthma was as bad as it was because of their fully justifiable worry over their father's health.

Life for me was nothing but transporting someone to the hospital or to school. Brett's asthma did not allow me even one night's uninterrupted sleep. I was washing, cooking, cleaning. There was very little joy around, and without some merriment in my life, I lost any sense of my worth. That compounded the unlikelihood of finding much enjoyment in my life. It was not until years later, many years later, that I realised that my life had been worthwhile; in fact, I was the very thread that held everything together.

The following are comments on the day from class members:

'In 1945 average wage was one guinea, which was one pound and one shilling.'

'We made all the clothes for the family, including PJs and dressing gowns. There were no Target or BWs until the 1970s.'

'Mother sent me to the little corner store. When I came home, I had a penny, half-penny change. Mother said, "The shop owner has given you too much change. Go back, and tell him." I did this, and the shop owner said, "Thank you for your honesty."'

Second Story

Things that calm my mind and soul

Arriving at Lemon Tree Passage, twenty minutes out of Newcastle, we began our three-part holiday.

I was now sitting on the veranda of our cabin. It was a barmy afternoon, and the water was rippling on the Lemon Tree Passage's waterway. A kookaburra lands just feet in front of me; other birds were flying swiftly through the gum trees. We and the birds were feeling free and letting life just happen around us.

A few days later, we were in Old Bar, staying with friends. Firstly, let me tell you how early in 2010 these friends, who lived on two and a half acres, came upon this little kookaburra who couldn't fly; they fed him each day. After they returned home from being in Melbourne early in June 2010, he wasn't there. They were disappointed and hoped he was all right. At the end of June, we stayed with these lovely people for a week.

One morning, I looked out of the window, and there was Kooka having a tug of war over a bone with one of their dogs. Claude and Leone were so thrilled that he had returned. Not being able to see anything wrong with his wings, they took him to a vet, who informed them somebody had clipped his wings and that kookaburras didn't grow new wings till June. The next morning, we arose to a nice cup of coffee, and as we sat outside, Kooka was sitting in the tree. He could fly a bit now. He did the longest flight they had seen—about forty yards. He was not very high off the ground, which I was sure he did for self-preservation, as he sort of had crash landings.

As we sat there at the table, Kooka was up in a tree branch twenty feet up. He went from the ground to the garden table, where the cat was sitting (they didn't take any notice of each other), then to a low branch, and then to the higher ones. Birdseed was put outside on most days for other birds waiting in the tree. There were two mud larks, two rosellas, (they ate one after the other, each one looking left and right while the other feeds to make sure their partner is safe), two pink-crested cockatoos, and a trill. The pairs of birds take turns at eating from the one of the three feeding bowls.

The mud larks had the most beautiful, crystal-clear little song. Claude could whistle a similar tune, and they would answer him. Leone called Kook with 'Kook, kook', and the kookaburra would answer with a guttural chat. Although Kooka had been alone since rescued over a year ago, other kookaburras would come and visit him every day, so one day he might fly away. They said a mother kookaburra, when she brought back food for the young, she would not feed them until each of them attempted to sing.

That was in 2010. By May 2012, the kookaburra did learn to fly and did disappear for quite a while, but then he returned with friends—another five kookaburras. He went down on to the table which he was fed from, as if to say, 'I'm the one.' But then another kookaburra, knowing he'd get fed with pieces of meat, jumped down on to the table, as if to say, 'No, I'm the one. Feed me.' Then another kookaburra jumped down as if to say, 'It's not them. I am the one.' They all got some food, but only 'the one' ate from our hands.

Leone, Claude, and I were having coffee with our toast and other goodies while Brett hand-fed the kookaburra. I was sitting there, soaking up the peace and beauty of the property, the birds, dogs, and cat. Here there were trees and grass and bare rock, and even the sky seemed different, bluer, less tortured by civilisation. My spirit was refreshed.

Negative space

Think of a picture of the sea with a pier and a boat. It has the boat and pier on one side, with just water on the other side, many would say surely that is negative space, it's just water in half the picture. However let's think about covering up what we call negative space. Now the picture is good but it doesn't look complete, is negative space really necessary to complete the whole picture. In music it is the negative space, the space and pauses between the note that really accentuate the music. I considered myself negative space when I went to do the course at adult education.

Re inventing myself

I could, tell you how I grew up on a market garden, or that I have 3 sons, or that my Husband died of cancer, or that I lived in New Guinea for 6 years, but I'd, rather tell you about the turning point that got me to where I am today. Though I didn't realise it at the time, it was attempting things outside my comfort zone that has made me, More confident, more daring, able to face whatever life throws at me. I had felt like a negative space inside this vast ocean of life.

Several years after my husband died, after most of bringing my sons Greg, Paul and Brett up, my life was full of uncertainties. Which is what happens, when life seems to be dealt out in sad chapters. With my three boys and endless, household responsibilities, **my life** seemed to have come to a monotonous routine. There were stumbling blocks that were causing me to be at a standstill.

1. I didn't have specific goals or dreams to believe in.

2. I had lost my confidence and self-esteem

3. I needed to face my fears and uncertainties

I decided to do a course at Adult Education, but what course. I looked down the list and thought, "I can't do any of these," My personal confidence was shot, but then I saw one called - "Stepping Stones" It went for 10 weeks, for beginners – that was me. On the second week, with 15 women sitting around the room facing each other, the teacher asked. "On a scale of 1 – 10 what would be your stress level be?" Going around the room there were 8's, 7's, 9's. and 6's. When it got to me I said 3 – nobody else was below 5. I went home thinking "I'm not in such bad shape after all."

A couple of weeks later we had a different teacher, a yoga teacher. She wanted to know our names and where our stress was. Well some had it in their shoulders, some in their back, or their stomachs – you name it, they had it. It came around to me and I said "I'm Jan and I'm fine. Several women came up to me afterwards and said, "How do you do it?" I went home thinking " **I'm in pretty good condition you know."**

The last week the teacher wanted us to share something that had happened during our course. I said "Last week when I came I had worn a scarf," as during that week I'd had, an operation on my neck. But this week I was able to say I was alright. Several women again came up to me asking how I could be so strong, they wished they could be Like me. **I left that course feeling ready to conquer the world.**

I wasn't going to sit around for the next 10 years walking placidly between the stumbling blocks neither knowing victory or defeat.

People need to understand that no one is playing with marked cards; sometimes we win and some times we loose. Don't expect to get anything back, don't expect recognition for your effort. Don't expect your genius to be discovered or your love to be understood. Complete the circle, complete something you are trying to do, not out of pride, or arrogance, but simply because you want to try. Close the door, on what you don't want, change the record, clean the house. Stop being who your were and become who you are

I changed who I was, I saw that I wasn't just negative space, that there were qualities about me worth exploring further, but it didn't alter the fact that I lost a lot of the confidence I gained, but I knew it was there and at a later date I built on it

Weeks went by, it was a case of, **"I'm OK"**
But after more weeks and months it was **"I'm OK…..aren't I?"**
I needed others' approval to be sure I was OK

I thought I was negative space, but all the time I was learning, the negative space was changing, just as the sea my sometimes have the boat in the negative space, that changes it.

I was changing… but my personal ego, never really felt safe.
The ego is very insecure, because it has no lasting worth, more often than not it self destructs.

But ……. then………. that's another story.

Maybe I shouldn't have done it

Hair dryer at beach in NZ -

While holidaying in New Zealand on a bus tour near Wellington, we ended walking on a beach it was a misty rain descending on us, not enough to worry about but on returning to the ladies room I saw that the hand dryer was blowing with great gusto, so I held my head under it to dry my hair. Absolutely horrified when I looked in the mirror I looked like Methuselah

Cracker in Spouting

Many years ago when living in my past house, we had a dog next door, this dog barked incessantly if they went out, one night when I just couldn't take any more, I carried out the plan which I had contemplated many times with this barking dog, I had shelved the plan of putting a sleeping tablet inside a piece of chocolate, but proceeded with my second plan as I sidled up to the fence armed with matches and a fire cracker, I lit the fire cracker and threw it over the fence as hard as I could, well – it landed in the spouting of their garage, it exploded with an enormous bang probably the surrounding spouting making it sound louder, I had never contemplated it landing in the gutter of the garage, needless to say it hadn't dawned on me the fact that I could have burnt down the garage – but the dog did stop barking. I triumphantly went back inside, but I won't do it again

Volcano exhibition

At Penshurst near Halls Gap, we went to see the 'volcano exhibition' which included a 20 minute movie on the action at the 2010 Iceland Volcano. The whole exhibition was so interesting. There were also all types of rocks there; it was explanations the differences and volcanic variations, like the holes in rocks which had been actually gas bubbles in the rocks, as they were being propelled explosively from the volcano the gas was released. In a room connected to the main room, there were rocks which you were allowed to touch, well of course, I did, and when I touched a rock it fell against another rock, it hardly made a sound as it was just a gentle touch, but when I quietly swore (I said 's--t'), that word echoed off the walls and bounced of the ceiling, in the stillness of the room, the impact of that word, now beyond retrieval hung in the air,- an eerie silence descended on the room. We left no long after that.

I was pushed off my shelf

High School

As a girl of thirteen, I did not feel very attractive and really lacked in personal power. If I could have been popular, I would have: I was trying to desperately fit in with others, I had gone through state school ignoring the beat of my own drummer and trying to dance to a tune I couldn't hear.

Growing up in our happy secure family was good but the consequences were that I didn't learn to take risks. I didn't know how to have the courage to shape my own environment. One of the underlying problems was that somewhere before the end of grade one I had been involved in a car accident, sustaining a broken leg and a fractured skull and spent months in hospital. This left me having forgotten I had ever been to school before, and not remembering any thing I had learnt during that time, so Primary School was not a happy time.

I enjoyed High School much better; I enjoyed the different subject, the different teachers. I no longer had to pretend to be interested in utterly pointless subjects; they now seemed to be insightful and interesting bits of information. Instead of the teachers voice droning on, it changed with each teacher, each had there own technique with different voice variation or phrases that set them apart, and my school work soared to heights, it had not reached before.

I was happy, I had found a safe secure shelf to put myself on. I was going to sit on my shelf, I was contented with how life was going............... But fate intervened.

Bentleigh High School started the year I started. I had been keep back in state school, so therefore I was amongst the few oldest in the school. The few of us older ones were spurred on in sport in school, so as to represent the school in the next age group in inter school sports.

The thought of representing the class or the school, in sports wasn't an idea that **flashed** like a lit up bulb in my head it was more like the sports teacher lighting a candle, and me blowing it out continuously, not wanting to venture off my little shelf. There was running races, swimming races, basket ball and tennis. This was a challenge that plagued me right through high school

This was pressure, like I had never known before, and I surely wasn't old enough to understand that pressure, can force you to make a step forward, it was somewhere I didn't really want to go. But I soon stopped worry about the weight of responsibility gathering around me, I was enjoying myself. At the time it was spurring my body and mind into action to meet the requirements of athletics, becoming stronger.

The once feeling of standing along side and apart, was disappearing into becoming part of a team. Though before this time I had not considered myself an athlete. I now looked forward to each day, ready for the new day to march in over the horizon. Even in the winter when riding to school, the icy wind, trying to freeze my gloved hands to the handlebars. Face and feet frozen, the only thing keeping any warmth in my body was my beret pulled over my ears, my socks pulled as high as they could go, and my legs peddling as fast as they could.

These high school years were good, exciting in a way that my life hadn't been before. I became bolder and freer. I was doing far better in my school work, I became a prefect in form 3, though to this day I don't know why people would have voted for me, in fact that year at graduation one boy and one girl got the citizenship prize for the year, When I was called up and receive the prize, well....I didn't under stand what is was or know why I should have got it.

This not understanding, not really believing or being able to acknowledge,100%. I now realize in later life, that this is an attitude I've carried with me most of my life. It was like, climbing a ladder getting up to the 8th rung, saying "thank you" and climbing down to the 4th rung, thinking that's where I really belong, and popping back on my shelf. Because many times I was receiving more attention than I could comfortably accommodate.

But I became like a cartoon I read in the paper many years ago it was called Fearless Fly

Fearless Fly, was this wimpy little fly with a miserable look on his face he would be half heartedly flying around the room. Then he would spy this matchbox, fly straight to it and go inside the matchbox. When he came out the other side he was empowered he flew with confidence, wearing a cape that fluttered behind him. He was ready to take on the world.

My cape got rained on sometimes, and I'd fall to the ground and not really wanting to fly again. But once I had changed I couldn't go back to the time I did not believe that I could accomplish much, **my belief system had changed from 'I am nothing', to 'I can do something'. My belief system had to change because the backdrop of what I was doing had changed.** I don't even think I could find that shelf I had previously been sitting on

I literally became a different person. It was acknowledging my own personal power. This doesn't alter the fact that in later life, advancing leaps and bounds in my journey of life, to confront new experiences I still had to be pulled out kicking and screaming from another comfortable little shelf.

I never thought about it till typing this up but my parents must have been so proud of how my life was going.

I am so glad I was pushed off my shelf

The game of Life.

I find life is a lot like a baseball game. When I was young I was playing in the outfields, scoring some catches in life, but as I got older I learnt that life's more than the outfield, that you have to do some bating of your own. You're told, you know this little round ball you've been catching or trying to catch all your life, well the time has come when you actually have to – well – that slippery little round white ball has got to be hit with a round bat – REALLY

Tricky situations kept getting thrown at me but I'd hit back and the game went on. But every now and then life gives you a curve ball and I'd miss, I'd get bowled out. And it would be like "I don't want to play any more".

It was a curbed ball that was thrown to me when my husband got sick and 4 years later died, and I lost all interest in the game. I didn't want to play any more.

<u>I had 3 choices</u>

1. Play the game and – "make things happen"

2. Go back to the outfield – "and watch things happen"

3. Get out of the game, sit in the grandstand and – "wonder what happened"

My first choice was the "the grandstand," I was hardly able to function. I saw that the boys had proper food to eat and clean clothes to wear, but the music had gone out of my life. However it became necessary to play in the outfield as there was Brett to take to school, Greg was at Tech, Paul was at State School. Greg and Paul also played football, there were lots of things to do running a house hold, and lets not even think about all the paper work. It was all a pretty dull routine, being a mother, a taxi driver for the three boys, the washing, cleaning and ironing - I wasn't aware of it at the time but any routine was better for me, than sitting around doing nothing.

But I was not the only person in the game, Greg, Paul and Brett were in the game too, and what actually happens after having lived with illness for quite a while, although we're all feeling for John, we had stopped sharing our thoughts, each trying to protect each other, and then without realising it, we didn't really know any longer what each person was feeling. And although we all played the game of life, it was not played all that well for awhile there. It took time to rebuild our lives, with openness and trust.

Attempting Something New Doesn't Always Go Well

The Titanic sunk on April 15 1912 four days after setting sail on it first voyage. I thought I was sunk after 3 speeches of Toastmasters:-

When I first went to Toastmasters, I was very nervous but wanted to pursue it to strengthen my own 'self' First speech nervous second speech, no better, third speech went OK but got a spasm in my back when I sat down and the only way I could stop it was to stop breathing, and lets face it you can only do that for just so long. My evaluator that evening was someone visiting from another club he said "I believe what you said, and you believe what you said, but I'm not sure everyone would have. Next speech I want to hear the Lion roar, so every one will believe you" The next speech was a 'show what you mean' I had a huge piece of cardboard and has drawn, paint, had stick ons. To illustrate, the cause and effect of volcanoes. Well, even my Greg was impressed with it, (and that takes some doing) I went with confidence and presented my speech. I was shot down in flames by the evaluator, a senior person, he told me I wasn't meant to have a drawing I was supposed to have my arms flaying lot of movement demonstrating it. I went home in tears, even though other members had told me it was great I went home shatter. The next day I took pen to a large sheet of paper and drew it up into squares and every day for a month I drew a picture. 1st day a drawing of a lion, caption-'The lion roared and the lion got shot down', 2nd day a drawing of an angry lion, caption- 'The lion is very angry', this went on for nearly a month. I had many excuses for not changing, for remaining who I already was. What! Part with the old, in my life!, the old ways, routines, expectations, hurts. Me? I'm afraid of change – ......*what might I turn into,*... it's hard to visualise it being better, ...*I am comfortable as I am thank you.*

My life had just been rolling, but now, I found, what with firstly going to 'Adult Education, and then Toastmasters. My life became more like separate chapters, which sometimes necessitate leaving part of the old chapter behind, in fact big chunks behind?

If **I** really want to think something through, there is no better place for me than to be in a forest or just amongst nature. I saw that nature has to makes changes. The forest seemed to cope with it well, the grass dies in the dry summer, many trees lost their leaves, they stand there naked resting, waiting for the next chapter in their lives. They stand there bare but strong, with some weak old or sick branches falling off. The tree is not afraid of change. The new leaves will grow healthy and strong, growing from healthy branches. I wonder am I holding onto things that should be gone, thing that are getting in the way of new growth, cramping the new ideas, not allowing them to flourish as they should and sprout in new, undiscovered directions, new thoughts new plans, new dreams......a new path, a new talent, new pleasure.

But by the end of the month the captions had taken a determined nature and I wasn't going to let this one person stop me from going to Toastmasters. Last caption "Oh damn I've just talked myself into continue at Toastmasters". It would have been much easier to just stop going and not go through the stress of speeches, but the journey that eventuated out of returning has been exciting absolutely priceless. Not journey but journey's the directions my life has been since could never have happened if I hadn't have gone through the stress of trying to improve myself.

But then when pondering why I seem to be almost, afraid of advancing, I tried to work out why.

> I drew a picture of a two story house, on the bottom floor I put my, worries, failures, hesitations, my doubts about myself.

> On the top floor I put my accomplishments, my achievements

> I mentioned to someone what I had done and said I seem to have doubts that hinder my advancement.

She told me when I came home to the house as soon as I stepped in the door, there was nothing positive, she told me to swap the floors around put the achievement on the bottom floor, so that when you enter your house your are immediately confronted with success. She was right it changed my mind set.

Tired but walking was needed

Having settled into our cabin which was to be home for the next 3 nights, Brett and I took a cup of coffee and surveyed the lovely view while sitting on the verandah of our cabin, it is a barmy afternoon and the water is rippling on the Lemon Tree Passages long water inlet. A kookaburra lands just feet, in front of us, other birds are flying swiftly through the gum trees. They look as though they are really enjoying themselves; it looks like they are playing a game. We are caught up in there activities, and it is giving us a serene sense of peace, and joy of just being alive.

After reading the Parks activities sheet, we decided to walk to the Lemon Tree Passage Bowling Club for dinner. It was only two kilometers but it seemed so much further, specially when we weren't a hundred percent where we were going, we were thinking we might turn back after the day began to darken, but then – we probably by this stage had further to go back than get to the club. Lucky they have a shuttle bus that takes you home, but we really felt we needed to have a good walk. For although the day had been hectic, it lacked any exercise, we had been spent the day sitting in a taxi, sitting in a shuttle bus, sitting at the airport, sitting on the plane, and lets not forget the other bus that got us here to Lemon Tree passage. It was a hectic but good day.

Love comes in many forms

Life is just a series of mostly forgettable events, unless we love – and love in as many different ways as we can from loving a person, to loving a book, a spirit, a place, an idea or a dog – to loving almost anything. These are moments when we feel connected to someone or something outside of ourselves and hold these moments in our hearts, in the presence of what matters, what we call **meaning.** All these connections lead to human moments. We hold these moments in our hearts, long after they occur, and feed on them when we are hungry for something to lift our spirits.

Men/Women have different views on Love

I took classes at a Retirement Village for a few years, one day on telling the stories, they had written Joan, told this lovely romantic story about how she met her husband to be, how that she thought he was nice as soon as she laid eyes on him, it was at a dance in Balwyn. Tom was in the navy and his ship traveled from Port to Port. A couple of months later Joan and her friends decided to go to a dance at Williamstown and what happened, Tom was there. Joan's heart did a flutter at the sight of him, she definitely had a few dances with him.

Off Tom went again, on board the ship. Later in the year Joan went to Coolongatta for a holiday, and what do you think happened, She bumped into Tom at the dance, Joan's heart was almost leaping out of her chest and she couldn't help thinking that this was some part of a vast eternal plan set for them. Their relationship really took hold, and as time passed many letters were exchanged and eventually they got married. Joan told this story to us with such remembered love, and satisfaction, and those of us listening couldn't help but go aahh.

But you see Tom was also a member of our writing group, and he looked quite dismayed. It wasn't that he didn't still love his wife dearly, but as far as he was concerned, they were just fluke meeting..........men

Sometimes we can fail to understand the love of the opposite sex, we can think a new jumper we bought is just gorgeous, where as he would think, it's OK. Where a man can be working with wood making a stool, really appreciating the texture, and grain in the wood, where as she thinks it will be good when it's eventually finished and painted.

I watched my little 5 month old granddaughter smiling and enjoying the moment. She was moments before just lying there relaxed and calm and then her mother came and said "hello" and her little legs kicked, her arms waved her fingers and toes were stretched. The joy she felt went through her whole being. Have we as adults forgotten how to feel the simple joy of living.

I asked my grandchildren what was there favourite day of the week, Tayla had a couple of days because of what she did on those days. But Jayden who is 10 said "Well Monday and Wednesday……and Thursday, actually I love everyday.

If I am in the mood I love gardening, I love reading, real life for the insight and inspiration of what the human body can do, with the inspiration of the spirit within.

I love reading novel too which are often inspired by life events, but then venture off to some exciting pace the writer wants to take you too.

I love the way the sun sneaks out from behind clouds and brightens up the whole day.

Just a trifle memorable event

We arrived at Coolongatta, then shuttled bused to the beach apartment. Not long after settling, the kids were in their bathers, the pool was on the 1st floor, above street level, groovy. The day was warm and the breeze around the pool was great. During this time Brett, Paul and Nat crashed, from lack of sleep the night before. At Tayla's insistence I went in swimming too. I had done 15 laps of this small pool, when an under school age child said "You can't swim very fast can you?" Lucky I didn't have a pin on me or his little floaties might have had just a wee accident. I proceed on and did 20 laps, then Tayla assured me that if I did another 10 laps I would lose 2 Kilos, so being ultra-intelligent I believed every word she said and did the extra 10 laps.

When everyone had awoken we went down stairs to the happy hour (cheap drinks) my two bicardi and cokes were very strong, but I was feeling rather happy. Paul and Nat went back to get the kids, on their return they found me very light headed, supporting the wall of the club, I was feeling great, but they wouldn't let me play in the traffic.

Animal who were my best Friends

When I was a child we had cats, probably because we had a market garden, and cats would take care of any mice problems. My brother and I each got a kitten, his was named Biggles and mine was named Berty, after the radio serial we used to listen to on the radio every Sunday night. Biggles wasn't around for too long but Bertie lived for 13 years, he was a member of our family. When I was little, playing with my dolls, he too would be dressed up in dolls clothes, a little dress and bonnet. Neither Bertie nor I were mature enough to realize the possible psychological ramification of this, I have a photo of him in the dolls pram lying with his head on a pillow with the blankets all tucked in around him. He was part of the family.

A bit over a year after I'd been married we went to live in Port Moresby in Papua New Guinea. We inherited a cat, with the house we moved into, this was not a friendly cat, it didn't trust anyone and wouldn't even let us pat it, it would, however, allow us to feed it.

The neigh bough over the road used to bring her poodle over, the cat would give it such a hard time. One day the cat sprang out of the bushes and attached itself to the poodle nose. We had one frantic dog running around the yard with a cat attached to its face. That was the last time the poodle visited us. The cat was not at all into the domestic way which was really spelled out to us loud and clear, when our little boy of nearly three standing at the back door said "look mummy pussy just did a little one". She gave birth to her kittens at the back door, they were obviously to be my responsibility as that was the last she had to do with them.

Many years later back in Australia, my husband decided the boys should have a dog – a dog, a friend of his, gave us this little Queensland Healer, now little Queensland Healers grow into big Queensland Healers. In the past I did not have any good memories of dogs. Our dogs name was Dino, and I never really gelled with him. We had a mutual respect for each other but there was definitely no bonding. I had never had a dog before. We did have him for quite a few years though. A couple of years after my husband had passed away we had trouble with him biting a few kids around the ankles, especially if they were riding a bike. Dino had come from a farm, so maybe kids on bikes to him were urban cows.

I said to the boys "If he bits anybody else I'm going to have to take him to the RSPCA". Well he did – so I did. I put his lead on, and got him in the car, I'm really feeling bad about this but I can't see any alternative. I had him on a lead as I took him down the path, at the RSPCA. I got to the door and the notice said "Go back to the street and go along to the next gate", oh great. So off we go again, back to the street, and go along to the next gate. When this young man came up to me and said, "Have you come to have your dog put down?" Now I am not feeling good about this whole experience, but now I'm feeling even worse. I look at this young man, who seems to have a permanent disability with one eye. He said to me "My dog just died, would you let me have him". With barely the pause of a breath, or a blink of an eye, I held out the Lead and said "His names Dino". And in a flash I was gone. Now that was a lucky dog.

Years later Greg who was not living at home any longer, bought an Italian Greyhound, which is a miniature greyhound, not a Whippet, like a miniature whippet. She would come and stay with me at the weekends, as Greg worked as a bouncer at a nightclub, he would get home at 3am and little Gina would be so happy to see him, that she would think it surely must be play time. This was the first dog that I really fell in love with. She eventually became our dog and Greg went to England to live. Little Gina would just love to sit beside me while I read a book and just so that I wouldn't forget she was there she would reach out with her paw and touch my hand. We would go for walks, I was taking her, but I think she was under the impression she was taking me for a walk, maybe she was. She would bark and let me know, if anyone was at the door, and felt very proud that she had known someone was there before I did. I guess her motto was 'To serve'. We had her for over 5 years, but she had an operation and developed a blood clot, and died.

To ease the emptiness this had left in our life. Brett and I decided to get another Italian Greyhound. When we went to look for a dog, we were looking for a little female, as they are possibly not so boisterous, but then we saw" Shadow" and forgot about the female.

This dog we were going to train better. He was going to know that dogs live outside, a lot of the time, most of the time. When I went out Gina had, had access to the house, but sometimes I would lock her out, she would look at me as if to say "If this is what you would do to a dog – man's best friend – imagine what you would do to a cat, maybe it too horrible to think about." This dog is going trained better than Gina, he was not going to look at me with his big brown eyes, no he was not going to look me straight in the eyes, when he did something wrong and reason with me that rules are meant to be broken, he was not going to tell me that the word "No" had many variations. We had Shadow for just over 5 years and he developed the same liver problem that Gina had, the Vet said not to get another dog from that breeder.

It was a few years before we got another dog, but now we have Benji who is a Cavoodle, which we have had for 5 years and a cat we have had for over 3 years, they are the best of friends. The dog has taught the cat that you do not wake me up in the morning. The exception being if I should wake up with her walking all over me then I know that means. 'I've been out in the rain I'm all wet and need drying. And no I have not managed to teach Benji that dogs live outside, nor have I taught him that "no" has only one meaning

I still believe that I am the boss of the house and they let me pretend that I am.

Authentic Power

We have 5 seances that make our lives very interesting.

We can 'hear', some people like music, teenagers like loud unpredictable music, many adults like Beethoven, many like opera, and then those who like to dance like rhythm music, children like nursery rhymes. A lot of boys and some girls like drums, and other loud sounds. Those who like motor sports, like the roar of the car engines. Calm people often like the sound of the sea, or the rustle of the leaves in the trees.

Then we can 'see', which stimulates our thinking, particularly reading, but then there is TV, seeing the family around the kitchen table, seeing the animals that live with us. Then there are the clouds in the sky, our gardens and our friends

Our third sense if 'Touch', there is the hard touch of a grab a soft touch of a butterfly, a fast touch of a typist, as her fingers fly over the keys. Even rain touching your skin.

Then there is 'taste' we can really enjoy that when we are eating something we like. It might be something sweet or bitter, spicy or sour, our own personal taste will let us know whether we like it or not.

And the fifth sense is 'smell,' I love the smell of roses, I hate the smell of ammonia, I like the smell of a meal being prepared, I don't like the smell of dog food.

It is all the experience of these senses, that make up my Universe, my world.

But it doesn't end there, these are all senses that influence me from the world outside me
I change the importance of these outside influences, by what I think, then I am bringing into action my **authentic power**. My

thought – emotions – actions – values – multi sensory or extra sensory perception.

It is these seances that cause us to be so different, it does not make us wrong in the way we are thinking – but other people sometime may not completely understand us – but that's their problem.

I would, like you to use your imagination, today I want you to imagine something like the story below:-

Explaining a Lawnmower to an alien

Me:- This is a lawnmower, we use it to cut the grass

Alien:- How do you use it

Me:- You walk behind it and guide it and it cuts the grass, with these blades whizzing around

Alien:- What makes the blades whiz around.

Me:- Well we get this fuel from a shop or garage that makes the lawnmower work

Alien:- Is it free

Me:- Oh no we have to pay for it, it has a thing called petrol in it that comes from oil and that does cost a bit of money.

Alien:- Why

Me:- Well you see, a lot of our oil comes from around the other side of the world, so it costs money to dig it up and export it here. Even though we have many oil wells off our coast, it seems better for the Government to trade our oil to other countries, and we buy our oil for someone else, I have a sneaking suspicion that it has some thing to do with all the countries being able to charge more money for oil.

Alien:- does it have anything to do with the pollution of the earth.

Me:- Oh Yes, but that's progress, you have to keep up with the times. I mean I don't have it going for long, and it's what society expects, I mean my neighbour has one, so I must have one too.

Alien:- Do many people have one.

Me:- Oh just a few million.

Alien:- Wouldn't it be easier to have a goat

Me:- Oh no, you see our councils wouldn't like that, they are very strict on what animal can be kept in suburbia, it would be a backward step in evolution. Then we wouldn't be buying petrol to run them or, buying new lawnmowers, they only make them to last for a certain time you know. And then there are all the people who make the parts, for the lawnmower, it keeps a lot of people employed, that means they earn money.

Alien:- What do they need money for

Me:-Well they might need to buy a lawnmower......it's complicated.

Our Feelings are Masks

Let's look at masks we wear....:- **Anger, Jealousy, manipulation, justification, shock, love, and Intelligence.** Today I'm concentrating on **Anger**

I'm not saying don't ever get angry, it's part of living. Lets pretend all these different faces, our feelings are hanging from a mobile, but also have rooms in your subconscious.

Greg had a lovely little miniature greyhound dog which he'd leave with me at the weekend. Because at the time at weekends he was a bouncer at a night club and he would get home at 3.am, Gina would think, 'Oh good it is play time" Not Greg's thoughts at all. Now if someone were to say to me 'Oh I couldn't stand a dog like that' I could get really annoyed and think how dare she say that. I would be **angry** and allow her words to control my thoughts, if I did that, I would have felt depleted of energy. But I replied "Oh but I love her". My love for Gina has made that persons thoughts - **irrelevant**.

The expression of love gave me enjoyment and strength. My good feeling couldn't be altered by someone else's words. The mobile becomes more balanced', my life became more balanced, we will be constantly adjusting the balance because the world, is not just good or bad. After getting a bad evaluation to a speech I made when I belonged to toastmasters, it was only my 3rd speech, I was very inexperienced. I was very angry. I didn't want to acknowledge the anger and humiliation I felt so it was like I banished anger to his room in my subconscious. But eventually he (**anger**) came out and he was wearing a cast iron suit with large spikes sticking out of it. He pointed his bony finger at me saying "Who do you think you are neglecting me" You were furious after you got home, humiliated at the harsh evaluation" He said "When I gave you a headache, you took an Asprin so you couldn't feel it."

It was true I thought. **Anger** said "You didn't have the courage to tell him, how you felt, you didn't tell others as you thought they would think you were being petty and turn away for you". Yes I thought I was enraged inside but tried to cover it up. It was right of you anger to make all that noise. Sometimes I am quite deaf to my thoughts, I am often worried I will hurt peoples feelings it I tell them I am **Angry**, and they will think I am making a big deal out of nothing, but now I know I only cut down on my own energy.

Acknowledging this **Anger** is beginning to feel satisfied, that it has been acknowledged, and calms down. However other feeling, like **justification** step forward and says how can something you put such effort into be bad, so much effort and time went into it, even Greg said it was good, to have him say that was amazing.

The anger had raged with in me but eventually **Intelligence** steps forward, and said "You can except this without being crushed, it was one person's opinion, others told you it was good, you know he was hash because the requirements of the 3rd speech was to show what you mean, and you showed with visual aids, whereas he wanted you to show it with movement. Don't worry it's your 3rd speech you're still learning. You don't have to pretend that you're happy if you're angry, you may think that being happy all the time would be perfect, but it would lead to boredom. Differentness can be difficult, but it also holds the key to a lot of locked up energy and experiences that make life exciting and fulfilling. But when you are feeling sun shiney inside let it show through the outside".

I've only touched on a few of the faces that are part of us but if we unite, using intelligence and love we can conquer many situations. Though, we can have a real battle going on in our minds, if we have joined Jealousy, anger and manipulation it can be very destructive. Don't think it is easy; **anger** can be so strong, that it can send **love** scurrying back to her room and **intelligence, well** it just walks away shaking its head, knowing you are not going to listen to it.

What makes me Tick

Well, once upon a time I **existed,** and that was enough, but with two of my boy having spread their wings and flown the coop, this allowed me to cast aside the cloak of cook and carer, and to discover who **I am,** what is my purpose in life.

I went to Toastmaster quite a few years ago, and having completed the levels to be achieved, there was one more thing I had to do for my final certificate, and that was, do something in the community. For a term I went into a state school one day a week with two other people, to teach "Public Speaking and Personal Development." I continued to run this course even when the other two people pulled out. At first I found it quite daunting, however after a couple of year I could see how good it is for grade 6 students. Like when a boy come up to me in the playground and said "I can speak to strangers now without going red in the face" Another boy whom I had chosen to be 'the Chair" (This person runs the session) did a nice confident job of it and came up to me after the session and said "Thank you for the privilege of being the Chair" I later said to his teacher, 'how nice of him to make the comment." She said "I can't believe he ran the session," she said "He's usually so shy he walks around with his head down hardly speaking to anybody."

What is involved with the course, is that all students have to do three, three minute speeches, one on 'themselves', one on 'what their main interest is', and the last one on 'anything' but it is to incorporate, voice variety, have a beginning, middle and end in their story, even some actions. Each week every student in the class has some part in the program, if not doing a speech they will be doing impromptu speaking, timing, evaluating or running one of the segments in the session. The course has a very levelling effect on the class, each student is talking about themselves, and the students gain more respect for each other, as they learn how, perhaps some peoples lives are not so easy. Many find a strength and courage they have not embraced before. Some of the students who were middle of the road students even struggling give some brilliant speeches and ever end up being in the Graduation night.

One school I was at on the actual graduation night a teacher came up to me and said "What do you mean Judy is giving a speech. I had her last year she didn't speak to anyone all year." Judy's class was not the brightest class in the school, but she gave a sweet, speech, not trophy winning material but she spoke in front of a large room of people, she may slip back, but she and the teacher now know she can do it. Many a time a teacher, has said "I didn't know they had it in them" One teacher said. "We're teaching them lots of things they need to know but you're teaching them how to live life."

At the end of the term there is a graduation night, where the best two speakers from each class compete against each other, there are trophies, and there are usually over a hundred parents come to participate in the evening..

Nearing the end of the course in term two this year, as I was leaving the secretary said "Do you want a pat on the back" I just looked at her, I didn't have a clue what she was meaning. She said, The Principle from Brentwood College just rang and wanted to know "why are the students, from this school, apart from being academically excellent, why are they all so socially mature and confident." The principle was told it was because of my course.

Glen Waverley South Primary School have asked me to do the course for the last 8 year. As the course progresses over the term there is an awakening of a kind of knowledge that is not included in the education system.

They learn about authentic power this is past our 5 main senses, of see, hear, smell, taste and touch, it is more than all the things they learn at school. It's about the power of their thoughts, emotions, and actions, which leads to the value system they will each hold.

I am always asked to come in term 2 so the teachers still have 2 terms to get the best out of the students, who are now more confident and eager to pursue this new found confidence in their ability. It is like when I went to toastmaster there are levels to pass through, before you get it. You start off with

> <u>Unconsciously</u> - gets to - <u>conscious</u> - then to - <u>conscious</u> - Which
> Incompetence   incompetence   competence
>
> leads to - <u>unconscious</u>
> competence Where you don't even have to think about how to do it, you just know.

Now I am taking a group of older people on Wednesdays, this is also a delight, the stories they tell are so vivid, and alive. They are really enjoying recording events in their lives. They are writing their memories, the topic each week, sets off a spark, of recalling things they thought they had forgotten. I am so glad they are, as I know so little of my mothers life. We can think, I don't know how to do it, or my life isn't interesting, but believe me, their stories, are real, insightful, and funny. They all want to leave the stories for their children to be able to read.

These are the things that give my life a sense of purpose and fulfilment.

Awkward Situations -The Cold cold day

On the cold miserable day I drove along the open road my face looked like thunder. Years before John and I had a house at Alexander, which we had rented out. The first tenants, they had been great, but the next ones were a bit lax on paying the rent. Which would eventuate in them getting a letter from John, asking them to pay up or get out? They also knew that John was very ill. In one of these episodes of not paying rent, and then, not getting a letter from John, they came to the conclusion that John was no longer with us. They stopped paying the rent altogether. A few months went by before I bothered to look at the bank account they paid into. I had tried to ignore the situation as I didn't really want to deal with it. When I did look, sure enough nothing had been paid into the account. With the rates and other bills from the property to be paid, I had to do something. I sent a letter. Nothing happened. I could just imagine them getting the letter, then rolling around the floor in laughter, thinking she wouldn't do anything.

I hated the world that day, It should have been handled months ago, but life went on and with bringing up 3 boy, and other involvements, time evaporated. So more months went by, before I sent them a letter, telling them I was coming up on a certain date to collect the key, and they were to have moved out.

The day arrived, so I drove up to Alexander, feeling nervous and apprehensive on this daunting mission. And feeling very small in the grand scheme of the universe. The trip took over 2 hours, the road was good, and her car smoothly ate up the Kilometres, and the petrol. The day was cold and gloomy, not uncommon for August, the rain had stopped, but there was a sharp brisk breeze sweeping across the open paddocks. I drove through the solitary country side, lone gumtrees standing in open paddocks. They looked as sad and lonely as I felt. The sun shone for seconds as it moved from cloud to cloud, the clouds hung heavily over the land. I was listening to the car radio, playing one of the songs like "The worlds so mean to me." The weather, the music the scenery, nothing was helping how I felt. As I was going through a mountain pass, I saw a hawk. The wind swept across the open rolling hills, and the hawk cried out from the heart of the cloud. ....I had not always been this hopeless, at handling things, but being married to a capable good man, I had over the years, somehow, relaxed in his strength.

John had been the pivot around which I had turned and now he was gone. I had not realised, over the years with being married, caring for the children, and everyday responsibilities I had lost my, identity, and I still had not really discovered the strength of my real self.

Arriving in Alexander I found they had not moved out, they had no intention of moving out. They doubted my ability to follow through with my threat. I was, taken aback a little, as I had not really expected such open rebellion. I was prepared though, and handed them an eviction notice. They were to be out in three weeks. I was angry with them and angry with myself for not being able to handle this.

I went to the police station and explained the situation, and asked if in three weeks time if they could be present for the eviction. On the day Brett one of my sons had gone with me, though he was only thirteen.

Brett and I arrived at 10 o'clock to take the key. The tenants hadn't left but were in the process of getting their furniture out. The man, tall and arrogant, and his voice showed his contempt for me. His wife's roundness was emphasised by her shapeless dress; she looked at the ground and kept her feelings to herself. A bold sweep of lipstick on her narrow lips, was the first thing you noticed, maybe it was her attempt of power in her uneventful life. I spoke flatly, without emotion, and retained my composure, I stared at them speaking every word so slowly, distinctly, that nobody missed a syllable. I spoke with neither anger nor pleasure, it was just fact. The Police were there, they didn't do anything, just sat in their car, until the tenants had left.

After the tenants and the police had left, I shivered suddenly noticing the cold. Brett and I went inside and locked the door. We stood there with our backs to the closed door, pretending we were brave. It was like the whole house held its breath. I never knew silence could be so loud. We stayed the night, as tomorrow I wanted to see and Estate Agent about selling the house. With little more than sleeping bags to tide us over the night, we lay on the floor near the open log fire. Staring into the flames, I pondered on my day, what I had done was not very special, not particularly talented, but definitely a challenge. The fear I had dreaded was not as full of substance, as I had thought it was. It had been more of an illusion, I thought as I drifted off to sleep, in my sleeping bag.

Past the Wounding of the Soul

The sound of Silence

A couple of years after I had lost my husband from Cancer, I wasn't feeling very positive. I had my hands full with bringing up 3 teenage boys, life was full of disillusions.

They had told me if John's treatment worked, if the Kemo worked...... other people told me if Brett and Greg take this medicine, they wouldn't get asthma any more........and if Brett does these exercises he will learn to read. However it came to the point when I did not believe in if any more.

I really liked Roger Whittiker's song

> I don't believe in if any more
> If's an illusion, - if is for children
> If is for children building daydreams
> If I could have my time again,
> I'd take the sunshine leave the rain,
> If only time would trickle slow,
> Like rain that melts the morning snow
> If only....if only

Holding on to the attitude -'If' doesn't take you anywhere, it hold you where you are with no hope and then you feel like the Simon and Garfunkle song.

> "A deep and dark December
> I'm just looking out my window
> I am a rock I am an Island.
> Don't mention love.....

> If I hadn't of loved, I wouldn't have cried.
> I'm not letting anyone near me, friendship causes pain
> Just stay away from me, I am a rock I am and Island,
> A rock feels no pain…and an island never cries.

You can walk a long time with happiness and not learn a thing, but when sorrow strikes it is very silent. But oh you learn a lot. And although I kept my silence and didn't let people know what I was feeling, I don't think it did me any harm, if I had been telling others how I felt all the time, I would have been wallowing in a pool of self pity.

However I had created anchor to stabilise myself

1. A friend, to talk and have a cuppa with, someone I could trust.

2. Reading good books, and at the time that included the Bible, to stimulate my mind and to comfort my soul, I learned to set my goals higher, make my thoughts calmer, and my love, stretch a bit further. My relationship with God was stabilising. I can't prove that my beliefs are true or false – but I do know they work. They support me, make my life richer, make me a better person. It is my conscious choice it opens my mind to unlimited possibilities. Though my belief system has altered a bit over the years.

My 3rd Anchor was painting; I hadn't painted since school, but did appreciate the beauty in painting. It was a very interesting exercise. You know when I was in mental turmoil I would just rush around to keep myself busy all the time, and let's not forget the different directions my mind was going, because your minds not always where you are. But when I was painting I was there with myself, applying the paint my mind has to be 100% with what I was doing. I was then a complete person and it let my imagination run free.

My 4th anchor. To sing, this lightened the spirit within me. I made a tape of songs, which lightened the spirit within me. I made a tape of songs that I liked they were positive and uplifting. I played the tape a lot, although I could be feeling very negative I would be listening to something positive and uplifting

The Oxford dictionary defines the Word GRACE as

1. The free unmerited favour of God

2. The divine influence which operates in man to regenerate and sanctify and impart strength to endure trials and resist temptation.

3. That which renders the soul capable of performing a supernatural act, that which effects the end for which it was given

    And that is pretty much how it worked with me.

Years later, that time I was up in the cabin in the middle of nowhere, I remembered on waking at 7am one morning and finding the cabin quite cool I went outside to sit in the early morning sun. I was sitting on a piece of wood enjoying the stillness of the morning, being conscious of nothing except what was happening around me. I could smell the pink geranium that had somehow survived though it had not been cared for by anyone for many years. There were three little blue wrens flying within feet of me, also 2 fantails hopping around the ground very close to my feet.

A dragonfly casually drifted backwards and forwards. I could hear the birds singing at a distance including the occasional Kookaburra. To my left a pair of magpies strutted across the track, to my right a cat wandered out from between some distant cabins and lay down in a patch of sun to lick its paw. The leaves at times were gently rustling in the occasional breeze. I could hear the river down the hill flowing along. All of nature was in peace and harmony. That day as I sat on the hill, I had peace of mind, I realised the silence in my mind was in peace and harmony just as nature had shown me, up there on the side of the hill the big things seemed small and the little things – well they weren't there at all, I knew then that I believed in the sun even when it wasn't shinning, that I believed in love even though I was alone, and I believed in God even when he was silent.

I knew in the silence of that moment, I was not weak, but strong. I knew I was strong and in simplicity of heart, came contentment.

In the ancient legend of Camelot King Arthur took the sword "Excalibur" from the lady of the lake. The 'Excalibur' was silent power, it was not ego power. It came from the placid lake, meaning it came from serenity.

In the silence I learnt

4. That if I were to concentrate on negative thoughts, I would have negative results.

5. That the world of the "ego" is brittle, fragile and insecure. The ego always wants more. It never feels safe and it had no lasting worth. More often than not it…self – destructs

6. You can't create a brand new energy and stay where you are now. Strengthening your psychological and emotional attitude. Boosts your sense of well being.

7. It means facing your insecurities and fear and really looking at yourself, and maybe coming outside of the sounds of silence.

True Hero's of the world do good and then disappear.

The majority of parents I know fulfil the essential definition of a hero, which is someone who acts selflessly in favour of something beyond themselves. World leaders and famous people might be monuments of greatness, but parents are living embodiments of unconditional love, service and dedication. Parents are the grass roots of humanity. Offspring that turn out to be good citizens are something they have created - they didn't just fall out of the sky. However, having been down that path, I'm not sure if some of them don't just pop out and run a ballistic course in life.

<u>Frances</u> was a hero in our lives, she was and elderly lady we met her through Brett having an eye test to see if he was dyslectic. He didn't quite fit into the normal dyslectic sphere but he fell into it sometimes. We became friends, she invited us to her place and the three of us would play yartzy on the computer, many afternoons. She knew Brett was more capable then he was letting on, so we did thing that did not look like work to him but stimulated his mind. Frances was a retired Headmistress, she came out from England after retiring and having never been married, did not have an abundant amount of friends, only those she met through working. This included us. This was when I still had all my boys living at home, a hectic time of my life, probably about 6 years after my husband had passed, a time when my self esteem was more centred on survival, than achieving anything for myself. This was around the time I nervously joined "Toastmasters" a public speaking organisation. Though it was not bringing more pleasure, than pain, to my already stretched mind, it did take my mind into another direction. Frances encouraged me and we talked a lot, and talked in a way that I did not do with anyone else, about achieving things and wonderful things we learned in books. I'd grown up in a placid home, and the feelings were more about you existing and being happy, but not about achieving anything. I did not realise it at the time but she keep expressing how I was going to really grow through this "Toastmasters experience, which I surely did. Before her passing she had said I would be doing something like I am today. Teaching in schools and other

things I am doing today. This was years before it happened but she sowed the seed that grew within me.

Frances is one of the hero's that slipped into my life, made a difference and left. There were only about 10 people at her funeral, and we went back to a friends house and were each asked what it had meant knowing Frances on going around the room we each reflected on what she had meant to each of us. I thought she had been there to help Brett advance, it was only then at that moment, that I realised she did as much, and more for me. I learnt to more than exist but reach for the stars. She was a rare person, just an average looking older woman with grey hair. A person you would just pass in the street, but on speaking to her, she had a twinkle in her eyes like she had learnt how to make the most of life, she was not only older, but wiser.

Am unexpected acquisition

It all started with us going to visit someone camping, at Port Arlington. We had taken the dog, who had been in the car many times, but we had not considered a long trip might be too much for him. Before getting to Geelong he threw up. We had a nice day at Port Arlington, but coming home not far after Geelong, we hear him getting close to throwing up again, spotting a park not far ahead we pulling in and let him run around. The park had a little lake, and even a bridge to walk over it, it was quite pretty area. There where no houses for 100 yards, and then, there were really only factories.

Cars came and went while we were there. Just before we were leaving, two car with young lads pulled in, they didn't stay long, but when they left, there was this tiny little kitten sitting there. I said to my son "There a little kitten", I shouldn't have said it I just knew I shouldn't have. Brett wanted to take it home, and seeing it was so small and so alone we took it with us. When we got home, I was afraid for a few days the dog was going to eat it, for it was so small. But they began to accept each other. At night the kitten would lie a distance from the dog, and each night the kitten got a little bit closer, until eventually she was lying right against his stomach with the dogs legs at her head and tail, she had worked out how to have a nice warm night.

They are best of friends, they chase each other around the yard, if I take them out in the lane at the back and another dog comes along Benji stand right over the top of her with her head just sticking our below his chest, he looks at the other dog as if to say "Don't even think about it" It is impossible to take Benji for a walk without her coming too, this means that Benji isn't getting very long walks as I don't want her to learn to go too far from home, so we just go five houses to the left of the gate and then back to the gate and 5 houses to the right. Some times she complains going meow, meow, I just tell her she doesn't have to come, she can go back, but she never does.

When she comes in at night and I'm at the computer, she gives one meow to me, as if to say 'I'm home' If she gives another meow and just stands there next to me know it means 'I've been out in the rain so you'd better dry me if you don't want your bed wet."

They are happy and Brett and I are happy with them. We are quite contented with our acquisition

Take one room of the house and explain it as a stage setting.

This is from when I was a child

Stage setting

Right side of stage:- wall with window in it, through the window you can see a tree that grows cooking apples

Front centre stage:- a kitchen table

Left side of stage:- at the front left a doorway to enter, cupboards all along that wall going up to the ceiling

Along back of stage:- and ice box fridge, centre back, a combustion stove with a kettle on and an iron on the side brickwork right back a sink over a cupboard and a small water heater on the wall

Opens Scene

With three people standing around the stove, the damp wood hisses and spits, one lady with her fingers crossed, hoping the cake about to come out of the oven has risen or not be burnt, or not be uncooked, the man rubbing his hand together and licking his lips in anticipation, elderly lady sitting at table climbs to her feet but finding it impossible to articulate the turbulence current of thoughts, sits down again. She looks irritated at the cook, knowing full well, that the oven wasn't hot enough and the cake will be flat. Standing there with her apron on is the lady of the house looking apprehensive, one hand clutched against her chest the other, across her eyes, and she looks through the slits in her fingers, blood pressure rising from having people watching, the anticipated failure.

Two children (Barry and myself) with faces like thunder standing in the back right corner, one washing the dishes, the dishes clanging against each other as he puts than noisily on the sink, then myself drying the dishes with equal, animosity.

If you can keep your head when all about you are loosing theirs, it's quite possible you haven't grasped the seriousness of the situation.

Camping, again, the kids love it; I knew before we went away, there would be the usual frustrating hour to go through, with tempers flaring, then finally, the tents would be up.

Then we would be relaxed camped by the river side. The breeze is always exhilarating, as I sit in the deck chair surveying the view. The Ovens River is running along side our tents. The river is different every year sometimes it is low and slow, but this year it is high and swift. It is always very cold tough; the water comes straight from the melted snow in the mountains. My boys and their cousins spend nearly every day in the river riding their surf mats to the bend, then jumping off their mats, before they get swept down the river.

The trees are magnificent, having been here by the river for many long years. There are a few birds around, but not really many. I can see a very small nest in the Weeping Willow tree it is so small it could fit in my cupped hand; a tiny little fantail bird flies up into the sky and three little tiny heads peek out of the nest.

The weather had been hot but, there are ways of coping, the kids of course are in the river most of the time. I had my own plan I would get the li-lo over to the other side of the river where there were plenty of trees, then tie my li-lo to one of the trees with a rope, hop on the li-lo and floating on the river, there in the shade of the trees and read a book, what a life. The kids would walk 50 yards up the river and swing out on a rope then drop into the river after playing for a while, they would ride their surf mats down the river or sometime hold onto the end of each other's surf mats and float like a long snake down the river. This was how days were passed away, on our summer holidays on the river

Every year somewhere over the three weeks there was a bad thunder storm, we would see it coming, the black clouds rolling closer, and we'd hear the distant rumbling of thunder, all the adults checking their tents to make sure they are securely anchored. The kids and most of the adults are up in the general purpose room, Brett was now up there too, after I found he had been sitting in his tent which had blown over, I could just see this shape under the fold of canvas singing "Nobody loves me, everybody hates me, I'm going to eat some worms." By 5 o'clock the fierce winds had come, the sky that had been grey, was now turning an ominous purple-brown, the storm was about to sweep in. By night fall the storm has arrive.

From the general purpose room each year we would observe the most spectacular lightening displays. Probably the lightening is just as amazing when it happens in the suburbs, but one is not in the habit of sitting at the window watching it. Whereas when we are away we are in very close contact with nature.

Then it came the rain pouring down relentlessly coming on an angle, slapping the tents harder and faster until the rain ran together in a wash. The fierce wind, shaking the treetops and making an infernal racket, with the lightening flashing and crackling across or down from the sky, and then the rumble of the thunder peaking at a sound shattering bang.

Because of the force of the wind each of us tent owners making a dash to our tents occasionally, so I too in the dark of night race down to my tent to make sure all was well. The icily wind striking me with savage force, pressing against my face blowing my hair into my eyes, the gum trees groaning and bending in the blast of the wind there black trunks with spindly branches waving like dark fingers into the sky, the ground was made a mud pool by the pounding rain

But alas, I see the wind had gone in the window of the front of my tent, then it has ripped the front zipper open, and my tent looks like it's going to blow away, I grasped hold of the front metal pole. Let me remind you I am, in the middle of an electrical storm holding on to a metal pole! The wind is blowing a gale, the thunder and lightning all around, it wasn't the best, but this storm was on the outside, nothing compared to the storm that was going on inside me during the time John was ill.

In the morning there are quite a few branches lying around the area, and tents needing adjustments The River had washed away the embankment at the front my brother's tent. He and his family had to be warned not to come out of the front of the tent. Although there appeared to be a few feet of earth there in actual fact on stepping on to it the thin crust of embankment would have just collapsed and he would have fallen down the embankment into the river, we had to pull out pegs from the back of the tent for them to get out, and then move the whole tent.

I surveyed the surroundings, I looked at the willow tree, I couldn't believe it when the little tiny nest was still there with the birds in it.

Doing and unusual and strange thing

Sometimes when we go on holidays we have a new experience, in Northern NSW we had just that we went to the races. When it was suggested, I searched my brain for data concerning horse racing, but found it void. It was only the 3rd horse race they had experienced in the area, and it was really just a large open area probably some bodies paddock. Measured out to the proper size for races. It was the first time some of us had been to a horse race, but there were an awful lot of people who really knew what they were doing.

We needed to take our own chairs, there were hundreds of people there, and like us they had dressed in their fineries, even a little hat, we all strutted around with an air of confidence, like we knew what we were doing. The area for sitting and watching was pretty rough; but we all found a spot to prop our chairs and sat there with a glass of wine in hand, sitting there like we were experienced at this sort of thing. We had to watch where we were walking as there were many mud patches, and all the high heels worn by the ladies went home the worse for wear.

Instead of big pavilions like you imagine a race track to have, there were tents with all kinds of drinks and food. There was a bigger tent for the bookies, the area so full of people that you could hardly walk through. A long, long trailer was bought to by truck consisting of a dozen toilets and positioned behind the tents. There was a racing guide, which we could not understand, so of course but we did it our way. One race we would bet by the beauty of the horse, or another time by our favorite number or the horses name we liked, of course we didn't come home rich but at $2.50 a bet, we didn't come home much poorer either, really the whole day was quite riveting. When the horses before the race were paraded around the enclosure, before their race, we were mere meters away from them. It was exciting being so close to the horses they were so majestic like they really knew that they were the center of attention.

It was a fun day.

Against the odds – or it worked out better than expected

Back, at the age of 29 **Charles Darwin** thought about marrying, on a piece of paper divided by with a line down the centre he weighed the advantages and disadvantages

Against	For
Freedom to do what you like	children, constant companion, and friend in old age
Choice of mixing in any society	
Conversation with clever men at clubs	
No expense or anxiety of children	
No loss of time, by wasting time walking	
or talking with the wife	
Be able to travel the continent	
Or go up in a balloon	**Weighing it up….yes…..I'll get married.**

My Against all odds

You know, I didn't want to go to live in Papua New Guinea, I so wished, the authorities would find some hidden dark secret in our past that would prevent us from going. I was happy where we were at that present time, we had been married a not much more than a year and had just bought a house, which I loved, why oh why do men seek some exciting adventure in their lives.

My mother was crying as we left, I wonder if she had a premonition that something was going to happen. As 6 months later she had a stroke and after 10 days passed away. During that 10 day, though I came back from New Guinea, she was unable to speak or indicate what she wanted to say as it appeared her thinking was fussy. Then back to New Guinea, life was casual and relaxed at that stage, before children.

It was lonely being home as most people worked, so you couldn't just drop in and visit a neighbour. After a few months I got work and this was good and I met new people and enjoyed the work, we joined the church so met friends there too. A child was soon to come and life was good, with Greg. We went down to the beach many lunch times and John met us there, it was a most enjoyable stage in my life. Years later while still in N.G we went to Europe, and again my eyes were opened to different people, different customs, and different languages. Living in Australia I had been so naive, I mean I knew the Queen had a castle in London. But I did not know that England and Europe were littered with castles and cathedrals so beautiful the mind could hardly conceive. And to think they were built hundreds of years ago – most things built in Australia were little wooden hut, and houses How did this gap in intelligence occur?????? What with N.G and Europe and the countless experiences, I grew as a person, far more than I ever would have if we had remained in Australia. Before leaving Australia, I wanted to stay in the house we had bought forever – now I could go anywhere in the blink of an eye.

Waiting

Waiting is not something I am good at, waiting for a bus or a train, waiting at the doctors. Waiting for any appointments, no, waiting is not one of my best attributes.

However we had to wait for 3 hours at Newcastle Airport, **3 hours**. It is not a very busy airport; it was really only on the hour when a plane left that there was a bit of a flurry. The Jet star check-in girls weren't even there all the time. But you know with having to wait I noticed things I would not have noticed.

A Qantas girl walked past, her uniform was smarter and she looked as though she was in charge, as she strutted past her pig tail swinging from side to side it seemed to accentuate her sense of power. Mothers were securely holding the hands of their little children; a team of football player came in wearing their uniforms and sat quietly some playing cards around a table. Three people came in separately in wheel chairs they were traveling alone, they were braver than I would be.

A lady an airport employee came along with and enormous vacuum cleaner, there was a vast area of carpet, which was kept very, clean. She did her job with determination and contentment, this was her job, yes, she was doing an important job.

A trolley came out loaded mainly with bread for the food departments. I have never thought about where they stock the food at the airport before. A lady going through the doorway to the toilets, thinking it was a ladies screamed, as a man came out of the doorway she was about to enter, unaware that the doorway led to a corridor to go down, to find the ladies and men's. A couple of ladies commented on our art work we had done I had made a statue and Brett had made a pot plant holder. They were very interested as they were milliners, and were very interested in the fact that our work could go outside. They were making hats for Cup Day and said it would solve the problem of if it rains on their hats.

We saw big business men take big business walking strides wearing big business clothes, carry big business brief cases talking about big business affairs in big business voices

Yes we did have to wait 3 hours but it was a time to relax and watch the world go by.

Printed in the United States
By Bookmasters